TIME CRIME

TIME CRIME

H. BEAM PIPER

WILDSIDE PRESS

TIME CRIME

Originally published as a two-part serial in *Astounding Science Fiction Magazine,* February and March 1955.

Published by Wildside Press LLC.

PART 1

Kiro Soran, the guard captain, stood in the shadow of the veranda roof, his white cloak thrown back to display the scarlet lining. He rubbed his palm reflectively on the checkered butt of his revolver and watched the four men at the table.

"And ten tens are a hundred," one of the clerks in blue jackets said, adding another stack to the pile of gold coins.

"Nineteen hundreds," one of the pair in dirty striped robes agreed, taking a stone from the box in front of him and throwing it away. Only one stone remained. "One more hundred to pay."

One of the blue-jacketed plantation clerks made a tally mark; his companion counted out coins, ten and ten and ten.

Dosu Golan, the plantation manager, tapped impatiently on his polished boot leg with a thin riding whip.

"I don't like this," he said, in another and entirely different language. "I know, chattel slavery's an established custom on this sector, and we have to conform to local usages, but it sickens me to have to haggle with these swine over the price of human beings. On the Zarkantha Sector, we used nothing but free wage-labor."

"Migratory workers," the guard captain said. "Humanitarian considerations aside, I can think of a lot better ways of meeting the labor problem on a fruit plantation than by buying slaves you need for three months a year and have to feed and quarter and clothe and doctor the whole twelve."

"Twenty hundreds of *obus*," the clerk who had been counting the money said. "That is the payment, is it not, Coru-hin-Irigod?"

"That is the payment," the slave dealer replied.

The clerk swept up the remaining coins, and his companion took them over and put them in an iron-bound chest, snapping the padlock. The two guards who had been loitering at one side slung their rifles and picked up the chest, carrying it into the plantation house. The slave dealer and his companion arose, putting their money into a leather bag; Coru-hin-Irigod turned and bowed to the two men in white cloaks.

"The slaves are yours, noble lords," he said.

Across the plantation yard, six more men in striped robes, with carbines slung across their backs, approached; with them came another man in a hooded white cloak, and two guards in blue jackets and red caps, with bayoneted rifles. The man in white and his armed attendants came toward the house; the six Calera slavers continued across the yard to where their horses were picketed.

"If I do not offend the noble lords, then," Coru-hin-Irigod said, "I beg their sufferance to depart. I and my men have far to ride if we would reach Careba by nightfall. The Lord, the Great Lord, the Lord God Safar watch between us until we meet again."

Urado Alatana, the labor foreman, came up onto the porch as the two slavers went down.

"Have a good look at them, Radd?" the guard captain asked.

"You think I'm crazy enough to let those bandits out of here with two thousand *obus* — forty thousand Paratemporal Exchange Units — of the Company's money without knowing what we're getting?" the other parried. "They're all right — nice, clean, healthy-looking lot. I did everything but take them apart and inspect the pieces while they were being unshackled at the stockade. I'd like to know where this Coru-hin-Whatshisname got them, though. They're not local stuff. Lot darker, and they're jabbering among themselves in some lingo I never heard before. A few are wearing some rags of clothing, and they have odd-looking sandals. I noticed that most of them showed marks of recent whipping. That may mean they're troublesome, or it may just mean that these Caleras are a lot of sadistic brutes."

"Poor devils!" The man called Dosu Golan was evidently hoping that he'd never catch himself talking about fellow humans like that. The guard captain turned to him.

"Coming to have a look at them, Doth?" he asked.

"You go, Kirv; I'll see them later."

"Still not able to look the Company's property in the face?" the captain asked gently. "You'll not get used to it any sooner than now."

"I suppose you're right." For a moment Dosu Golan watched Coru-hin-Irigod and his followers canter out of the yard and break into a gallop on the road beyond. Then he tucked his whip under his arm. "All right, then. Let's go see them."

The labor foreman went into the house; the manager and the guard captain went down the steps and set out across the yard. A big slat-sided wagon, drawn by four horses, driven by an old slave in a blue smock and a thing like a sunbonnet, rumbled past, loaded with newly-picked oranges. Blue woodsmoke was beginning to rise from the stoves at the open kitchen and a couple of slaves were noisily chopping wood. Then they came to the stockade of close-set pointed poles. A guard sergeant in a red-trimmed blue jacket, armed with a revolver, met them with a salute which Kiro Soran returned: he unfastened the gate and motioned four or five riflemen into positions from which they could fire in between the poles in case the slaves turned on their new owners.

There seemed little danger of that, though Kiro Soran kept his hand close to the butt of his revolver. The slaves, an even hundred of them, squatted under awnings out of the sun, or stood in line to drink at the water-butt. They furtively watched the two men who had entered among them, as though expecting blows or kicks; when none were forthcoming, they relaxed slightly. As the labor foreman had said, they were clean and looked healthy. They were all nearly naked; there were about as many women as men, but no children or old people.

"Radd's right," the captain told the new manager. "They're not local. Much darker skins, and different face-structure; faces wedge-shaped instead of oval, and differently shaped noses, and brown eyes instead of black. I've seen people like that, somewhere, but —"

He fell silent. A suspicion, utterly fantastic, had begun to form in his mind, and he stepped closer to a group of a dozen-odd, the manager following him. One or two had been unmercifully lashed, not long ago, and all bore a few lash-marks. Odd sort of marks, more like burn-blisters than welts. He'd have to have the Company doctor look at them. Then he caught their speech, and the suspicion was converted to certainty.

"These are not like the others: they wear fine garments, and walk proudly. They look stern, but not cruel. They are the real masters here; the others are but servants."

He grasped the manager's arm and drew him aside.

"You know that language?" he asked. When the man called Dosu Golan shook his head, he continued: "That's Kharanda; it's a dialect spoken by a people in the Ganges Valley, in India, on the Kholghoor Sector of the Fourth Level."

Dosu Golan blinked, and his face went blank for a moment.

"You mean they're from outtime?" he demanded. "Are you sure?"

"I did two years on Fourth Level Kholghoor with the Paratime Police, before I took this job," the man called Kiro Soran replied. "And another thing. Those lash-marks were made with some kind of an electric whip. Not these rawhide quirts the Caleras use."

It took the plantation manager all of five seconds to add that up. The answer frightened him.

"Kirv, this is going to make a simply hideous uproar, all the way up to Home Time Line main office," he said. "I don't know what I'm going to do —"

"Well, I know what I have to do." The captain raised his voice, using the local language: "Sergeant! Run to the guardhouse, and tell Sergeant Adarada to mount up twenty of his men and take off after those Caleras who sold us these slaves. They're headed down the road toward the river. Tell him to bring them all back, and especially their chief, Coru-hin-Irigod, and him I want alive and able to answer questions. And then get the white-cloak lord Urado Alatena, and come back here."

"Yes, captain." The guards were all Yarana people; they disliked Caleras intensely. The sergeant threw a salute, turned, and ran.

"Next, we'll have to isolate these slaves," Kiro Soran said. "You'd better make a full report to the Company as soon as possible. I'm going to transpose to Police Terminal Time Line and make my report to the Sector-Regional Subchief. Then—"

"Now wait a moment, Kirv," Dosu Golan protested. "After all, I'm the manager, even if I am new here. It's up to me to make the decisions—"

Kiro Soran shook his head. "Sorry, Doth. Not this one," he said. "You know the terms under which I was hired by the Company. I'm still a field agent of the Paratime Police, and I'm reporting back on duty as soon as I can transpose to Police Terminal. Look; here are a hundred men and women who have been shifted from one time-line, on one paratemporal sector of probability, to another. Why, the world from which these people came doesn't even exist in this space-time continuum. There's only one way they could have gotten here, and that's the way we did — in a Ghaldron-Hesthor paratemporal transposition field. You can carry it on from there as far as you like, but the only thing it adds up to is a case for the Paratime Police. You had better include in your report mention that I've reverted to police status; my Company pay ought to be stopped as of now. And until somebody who outranks me is sent here, I'm in complete charge. Paratime Transposition Code, Section XVII, Article 238."

The plantation manager nodded. Kiro Soran knew how he must feel; he laid a hand gently on the younger man's shoulder.

"You understand how it is, Doth; this is the only thing I can do."

"I understand, Kirv. Count on me for absolutely anything." He looked at the brown-skinned slaves, and lines of horror and loathing appeared around his mouth. "To think that some of our own people would do a thing like this! I hope you can catch the devils! Are you transposing out, now?"

"In a few minutes. While I'm gone, have the doctor look at those whip-injuries. Those things could get infected. Fortunately, he's one of our own people."

"Yes, of course. And I'll have these slaves isolated, and if Adarada brings back Coru-hin-Irigod and his gang before you get back, I'll have them locked up and waiting for you. I suppose you want to narco-hypnotize and question the whole lot, slaves and slavers?"

The labor foreman, known locally as Urado Alatena, entered the stockade.

"What's wrong, Kirv?" he asked.

The Paratime Police agent told him, briefly. The labor foreman whistled, threw a quick glance at the nearest slaves, and nodded.

"I knew there was something funny about them," he said. "Doth, what a simply beastly thing to happen, two days after you take charge here!"

"Not his fault," the Paratime Police agent said. "I'm the one the Company'll be sore at, but I'd rather have them down on me rather than old Tortha Karf. Well, sit on the lid till I get back," he told both of them. "We'll need some kind of a story for the locals. Let's see— Explain to the guards, in the hearing of some of the more talkative slaves, that these slaves are from the Asian mainland, that they are of a people friendly to our people, and that they were kidnaped by pirates, our enemies. That ought to explain everything satisfactorily."

On his way back to the plantation house, he saw a clump of local slaves staring curiously at the stockade, and noticed that the guards had unslung their rifles and fixed their bayonets. None of them had any idea, of course, of what had happened, but they all seemed to know, by some sort of ESP, that something was seriously wrong. It was going to get worse, too, when strangers began arriving, apparently from nowhere, at the plantation.

Verkan Vall waited until the small, dark-eyed woman across the circular table had helped herself from one of the bowls on the revolving disk in the middle, then rotated it to bring the platter of cold boar-ham around to himself.

"Want some of this, Dalla?" he asked, transferring a slice of ham and a spoonful of wine sauce to his plate.

"No, I'll have some of the venison," the black-haired girl beside him said. "And some of the pickled beans. We'll be getting our fill of pork, for the next month."

"I thought the Dwarma Sector people were vegetarians," Jandar Jard, the theatrical designer, said. "Most nonviolent peoples are, aren't they?"

"Well, the Dwarma people haven't any specific taboo against taking life," Bronnath Zara, the dark-eyed woman in the brightly colored gown, told him. "They're just utterly noncombative, non-aggressive. When I was on the Dwarma Sector, there was a horrible scandal at the village where I was staying. It seems that a farmer and a meat butcher fought over the price of a pig. They actually raised their voices and shouted contradictions at each other. That happened two years before, and people were still talking about it."

"I didn't think they had any money, either," Verkan Vall's wife, Hadron Dalla, said.

"They don't," Zara said. "It's all barter and trade. What are you and Vall going to use for a visible means of support, while you're there?"

"Oh, I have my mandolin, and I've learned all the traditional Dwarma songs by hypno-mech," Dalla said. "And Transtime Tours is fitting Vall out with a bag of tools; he's going to do repair work and carpentry."

"Oh, good; you'll be welcome anywhere," Zara, the sculptress, said. "They're always glad to entertain a singer, and for people who do the fine decorative work they do, they're the most incompetent practical mechanics I've ever seen or heard of. You're going to travel from village to village?"

"Yes. The cover-story is that we're lovers who have left our village in order not to make Vall's former wife unhappy by our presence," Dalla said.

"Oh, good! That's entirely in the Dwarma romantic tradition," Bronnath Zara approved. "Ordinarily, you know, they don't like to travel. They have a saying: 'Happy are the trees, they abide in their own place; sad are the winds, forever they wander.' But that'll be a fine explanation."

Thalvan Dras, the big man with the black beard and the long red coat and cloth-of-gold sash who lounged in the host's seat, laughed.

"I can just see Vall mending pots, and Dalla playing that mandolin and singing," he said. "At least, you'll be getting away from police work. I don't suppose they have anything like police on the Dwarma Sector?"

"Oh, no; they don't even have any such concept," Bronnath Zara said. "When somebody does something wrong, his neighbors all come and talk to him about it till he gets ashamed, then they all forgive him and have a feast. They're lovely people, so kind and gentle. But you'll get awfully tired of them in about a month. They have absolutely no respect for anybody's privacy. In fact, it seems slightly indecent to them for anybody to want privacy."

One of Thalvan Dras' human servants came into the room, coughed apologetically, and said:

"A visiphone-call for His Valor, the Mavrad of Nerros."

Vall went on nibbling ham and wine sauce; the servant repeated the announcement a trifle more loudly.

"Vall, you're being paged!" Thalvan Dras told him, with a touch of impatience.

Verkan Vall looked blank for an instant, then grinned. It had been so long since he had even bothered to think about that antiquated title of nobility—

"Vall's probably forgotten that he has a title," a girl across the table, wearing an almost transparent gown and nothing else, laughed.

"That's something the Mavrad of Mnirna and Thalvabar never forgets," Jandar Jard drawled, with what, in a woman, would have been cattishness.

Thalvan Dras gave him a hastily repressed look of venomous anger, then said something, more to Verkan Vall than to Jandar

Jard, about titles of nobility being the marks of social position and responsibility which their bearers should never forget. That jab, Vall thought, following the servant out of the room, had been a mistake on Jard's part. A music-drama, for which he had designed the settings, was due to open here in Dhergabar in another ten days. Thalvan Dras would cherish spite, and a word from the Mavrad of Mnirna and Thalvabar would set a dozen critics to disparaging Jandar's work. On the other hand, maybe it had been smart of Jandar Jard to antagonize Thalvan Dras; for every critic who bowed slavishly to the wealthy nobleman, there were at least two more who detested him unutterably, and they would rush to Jandar Jard's defense, and in the ensuing uproar, the settings would get more publicity than the drama itself.

In the visiphone booth, Vall found a girl in a green blouse, with the Paratime Police insigne on her shoulder, looking out of the screen. The wall behind her was pale green striped in gold and black.

"Hello, Eldra," he greeted her.

"Hello, Chief's Assistant: I'm sorry to bother you, but the Chief wants to talk to you. Just a moment, please."

The screen exploded into a kaleidoscopic flash of lights and colors, then cleared again. This time, a man looked out of it. He was well into middle age; close to his three hundredth year. His hair, a uniform iron-gray, was beginning to thin in front, and he was acquiring the beginnings of a double chin. His name was Tortha Karf, and he was Chief of Paratime Police, and Verkan Vall's superior.

"Hello, Vall. Glad I was able to locate you. When are you and Dalla leaving?"

"As soon as we can get away from this luncheon, here. Oh, say an hour. We're taking a rocket to Zarabar, and transposing from there to Passenger Terminal Sixteen, and from there to the Dwarma Sector."

"Well, Vall, I hate to bother you like this," Tortha Karf said, "but I wish you'd stop by Headquarters on your way to the rocketport. Something's come up— it may be a very nasty business— and I'd like to talk to you about it."

"Well, Chief, let me remind you that this vacation, which I've had to postpone four times already, has been overdue for four years," Vall said.

"Yes, Vall, I know. You've been working very hard, and you and Dalla are entitled to a little time together. I just want you to look into something, before you leave."

"It'll have to take some fast looking. Our rocket blasts off in two hours."

"It may take a little longer; if it does, you and Dalla can transpose to Police Terminal and take a rocket for Zarabar Equivalent, and transpose from there to Passenger Sixteen. It would save time if you brought Dalla with you to Headquarters."

"Dalla won't like this," Vall understated.

"No. I'm afraid not." Tortha Karf looked around apprehensively, as though estimating the damage an enraged Hadron Dalla could do to his office furnishings. "Well, try to get here as soon as you can."

Thalvan Dras was holding forth, when Vall returned, on one of his favorite preoccupations.

". . . Reason I'm taking such an especially active interest in this year's Arts Exhibitions; I've become disturbed at the extent to which so many of our artists have been content to derive their motifs, even their techniques, from outtime art." He was using his vocowriter, rather than his conversational, voice. "I yield to no one in my appreciation of outtime art — you all know how devotedly I collect objects of art from all over paratime — but our own artists should endeavor to express their artistic values in our own artistic idioms."

Vall bent over his wife's shoulder.

"We have to leave, right away," he whispered.

"But our rocket doesn't blast off for two hours—"

Thalvan Dras had stopped talking and was looking at them in annoyance.

"I have to go to Headquarters before we leave. It'll save time if you come along."

"Oh, no, Vall!" She looked at him in consternation. "Was that Tortha Karf, calling?" She replaced her plate on the table and got to her feet.

"I'm dreadfully sorry, Dras," he addressed their host. "I just had a call from Tortha Karf. A few minor details that must be cleared up, before I leave Home Time Line. If you'll accept our thanks for a wonderful luncheon —"

"Why, certainly, Vall. Brogoth, will you call —" He gave a slight chuckle. "I'm so used to having Brogoth Zaln at my elbow that I'd forgotten he wasn't here. Wait. I'll call one of the servants to have a car for you."

"Don't bother; we'll take an aircab," Vall told him.

"But you simply can't take a public cab!" The black-bearded nobleman was shocked at such an obscene idea. "I will have a car ready for you in a few minutes."

"Sorry, Dras; we have to hurry. We'll get a cab on the roof. Good-by, everybody; sorry to have to break away like this. See you all when we get back."

Hadron Dalla watched dejectedly as the green crags and escarpments of the Paratime Building loomed above the city in front of them, and began slipping under the aircab. She felt like a prisoner recaptured at the moment when attempted escape was about to succeed.

"I knew it," she said. "I knew he'd find something. He's trying to break things up between us, the way he did twenty years ago.'"

Vall crushed out his cigarette and said nothing. That hadn't been true, and she knew it as well as he did. There had been many other factors involved in the disintegration of their previous marriage, most of them of her own contribution. But that had been twenty years ago, she told herself. This time it would be different, if only—

"Really, Vall, he's never liked me," she went on. "He's jealous of me, I think. You're to be his successor, when he retires, and he thinks I'm not a good influence —"

"Oh, rubbish, Dalla! The Chief has always liked you," Vall replied. "If he didn't, do you think he'd always be inviting us to that farm of his, on Fifth Level Sicily? It's just that this job of ours has no end; something's always turning up, outtime."

The music that the cab had been playing died away. "Paratime Building, just below," it said, in a light feminine voice. "Which landing stage, please?" Vall leaned forward and punched at the buttons in front of him. Something in the cab's electronic brain gave a rapid series of clicks as it shifted from the general Paratime Building beam to the beam of the Paratime Police landing stage, then it said, "Thank you." The building below seemed to rotate upward toward them as it settled down. Then the antigrav-field snapped off, the cab door popped open, and the cab said: "Good-by, now. Ride with me again, sometime."

They crossed the landing stage, entered the antigrav shaft, and floated downward; at the end of a hallway, below, Vall opened the door of Tortha Karf's office and ushered her through ahead of him.

Tortha Karf, inside the semicircle of his desk, was speaking into a recording phone as they approached. He shut off the machine and waved, a cigarette in his hand.

"Come on back and sit down," he invited. "Be with you in a moment." Then he switched on the phone again and went on talking — something about prompter evaluation and transmission of reports and less reliance on robot equipment. "Sign that up, my personal order, and see it's transmitted to everybody down to and including Sector Regional Subchief level," he finished, then hung up the phone and turned to them.

"Sorry about this," he said. "Sit down, if you please. Cigarettes?"

She shook her head and sat down in one of the chairs behind the desk; she started to relax and then caught herself and sat erect, her hands on her lap.

"This won't interfere with your vacation, Vall," Tortha Karf was saying. "I just need a little help before you transpose out."

"We have to catch the rocket for Zarabar in an hour and a half," Dalla reminded him.

"Don't worry about that; if you miss the commercial rocket, our police rockets can give it an hour's start and pass it before it gets to Zarabar," Tortha Karf said. Then he turned to Vall. "Here's what's happened," he said. "One of our field agents on detached duty as guard captain for Consolidated Outtime Foodstuffs on a fruit plantation in western North America, Third Level Esaron Sector, was looking over a lot of slaves who had been sold to the plantation by a local slave dealer. He heard them talking among themselves — in Kharanda."

Dalla caught the significance of that before Vall did. At first, she was puzzled; then, in spite of herself, she was horrified and angry. Tortha Karf was explaining to Vall just where and on what paratemporal sector Kharanda was spoken.

"No possibility that this agent, Skordran Kirv, could have been mistaken. He worked for a while on Kholghoor Sector, himself; knew the language by hypno-mech and by two years' use," Tortha Karf was saying. "So he ordered himself back on duty, had the slaves isolated and the slave dealers arrested, and then transposed to Police Terminal to report. The SecReg Subchief, old Vulthor Tharn, confirmed him in charge at this Esaron Sector plantation, and assigned him a couple of detectives and a psychist."

"When was this?" Vall asked.

"Yesterday. One-Five-Nine Day. About 1500 local time."

"Twenty-three hundred Dhergabar time," Vall commented.

"Yes. And I just found out about it. Came in in the late morning generalized report-digest; very inconspicuous item, no special urgency symbol or anything. Fortunately, one of the report editors spotted it and messaged Police Terminal for a copy of the original report."

"It's been a long time since we had anything like that," Vall said, studying the glowing tip of his cigarette, his face wearing the curiously withdrawn expression of a conscious memory recall. "Fifty years ago; the time that gang kidnaped some girls from Second Level Triplanetary Empire Sector and sold them into the harem of some Fourth Level Indo-Turanian sultan."

"Yes. That was your first independent case, Vall. That was when I began to think you'd really make a cop. One renegade First Level citizen and four or five ServSec Prole hoodlums, with a stolen fifty-foot conveyer. This looks like a rather more ambitious operation." Dalla got one of her own cigarettes out and lit it. Vall and Tortha Karf were talking cop talk about method of operation and possible size of the gang involved, and why the slaves had been shipped all the way from India to the west coast of North America.

"Always ready sale for slaves on the Esaron Sector," Vall was saying. "And so many small independent states, and different languages, that outtimers wouldn't be particularly conspicuous."

"And with this barbarian invasion going on on the Kholghoor Sector, slaves could be picked up cheaply," Tortha Karf added.

In spite of her determination to boycott the conversation, curiosity began to get the better of her. She had spent a year and a half on the Kholghoor Sector, investigating alleged psychic powers of the local priests. There'd been nothing to it — the prophecies weren't precognition, they were shrewd inferences, and the miracles weren't psychokinesis, they were sleight-of-hand. She found herself asking:

"What barbarian invasion's this?"

"Oh, Central Asian nomadic people, the Croutha," Tortha Karf told her. "They came down through Khyber Pass about three months ago, turned east, and hit the headwaters of the Ganges. Without punching a lot of buttons to find out exactly, I'd say they're halfway to the delta country by now. Leader seems to be a chieftain called Llamh Droogh the Red. A lot of paratime trading companies are yelling for permits to introduce firearms in the Kholghoor Sector to protect their holdings there."

She nodded. The Fourth Level Kholghoor Sector belonged to what was known as Indus-Ganges-Irriwady Basic Sector-Grouping — probability of civilization having developed late on the Indian subcontinent, with the rest of the world, including Europe, in Stone Age savagery or early Bronze Age barbarism. The Kharandas, the people among whom she had once done field-research work, had developed a pre-mechanical, animal-power, handcraft, edge-weapon culture. She could imagine the roads jammed with fugitives from the barbarian invaders, the conveyer hidden among the trees, the lurking slavers —

Watch it, Dalla! Don't let the old scoundrel play on your feelings!

"Well, what do you want me to do, Chief?" Vall was asking.

"Well, I have to know just what this situation's likely to develop into, and I want to know why Vulthor Tharn's been sitting on this ever since Skordran Kirv reported it to him —"

"I can answer the second one now," Vall replied. "Vulthor Tharn is due to retire in a few years. He has a negatively good, undistinguished record. He's trying to play it safe."

Tortha Karf nodded. "That's what I thought. Look, Vall; suppose you and Dalla transpose from here to Police Terminal, and go to Novilan Equivalent, and give this a quick look-over and report to me, and then rocket to Zarabar Equivalent and go on with your trip to the Dwarma Sector. It may delay you eight or ten hours, but —"

"Closer twenty-four," Vall said. "I'd have to transpose to this plantation, on the Esaron Sector. How about it, Dalla? Would you want to do that?"

She hesitated for a moment, angry with him. He didn't want to refuse, and he was trying to make her do it for him.

"I know, it's a confounded imposition, Dalla," Tortha Karf told her. "But it's important that I get a prompt and full estimate of the situation. This may be something very serious. If it's an isolated incident, it can be handled in a routine manner, but I'm afraid it's not. It has all the marks of a large-scale operation, and if this is a matter of mass kidnapings from one sector and transpositions to another, you can see what a threat this is to the Paratime Secret."

"Moral considerations entirely aside," Vall said. "We don't need to discuss them; they're too obvious."

She nodded. For over twelve millennia, the people of her race and Vall's and Tortha Karf's had been existing as parasites on all the innumerable other worlds of alternate probability on the lateral dimension of time. Smart parasites never injure their hosts, and try never to reveal their existence.

"We could do that, couldn't we, Vall?" she asked, angry at herself now for giving in. "And if you want to question these slaves, I speak Kharanda, and I know how they think. And I'm a qualified and licensed narco-hypnotic technician."

"Well, that's splendid, Dalla!" Tortha Karf enthused. "Wait a moment; I'll message Police Terminal to have a rocket ready for you."

"I'll need a hypno-mech for Kharanda, myself," Vall said. "Dalla, do you know Acalan?" When she shook her head, he turned back to Tortha Karf. "Look; it's about a four-hour rocket hop to Novilan Equivalent. Say we have the hypno-mech machines installed in the rocket; Dalla and I can take our language lessons on the way, and be ready to go to work as soon as we land."

"Good idea," Tortha Karf approved. "I'll order that done, right away. Now —"

Oddly enough, she wasn't feeling so angry, now that she had committed herself and Vall. Come to think of it, she had never been on Police Terminal Time Line; very few people, outside the Paratime Police, ever had. And, she had always wanted to learn more about Vall's work, and participate in it with him. And if she'd made him refuse, it would have been something ugly between them all the time they would be on the Dwarma Sector. But this way —

The big circular conveyer room was crowded, as it had been every minute of every day for the past ten thousand years. At the great circular desk in the center, departing or returning police officers were checking in or out with the flat-topped cylindrical robot clerks, or talking to human attendants. Some were in the regulation green uniform; others, like himself, were in civilian clothes; more were in outtime costumes from all over paratime. Fringed robes and cloth-of-gold sashes and conical caps from the Second Level Khiftan Sector; Fourth Level Proto-Aryan mail and helmets; the short tunics and kilts of Fourth Level Alexandrian-Roman Sector; the Zarkantha loincloth and felt cap and daggers; there were priestly vestments stiff with gold, and military uniforms; there were trousers and jackboots and bare legs; blasters, and swords, and pistols, and bows and quivers, and spears. And the place was loud with a babel of voices and the clatter of teleprinters.

Dalla was looking about her in surprised delight; for her, the vacation had already begun. He was glad; for a while, he had been afraid that she would be unhappy about it. He guided her through the crowd to the desk, spoke for a while to one of the human attendants, and found out which was their conveyer. It was a fixed-destination shuttler, operative only between Home Time Line and Police Terminal, from which most of the Paratime Police operations were routed. He put Dall in through the sliding door, followed, and closed it behind him, locking it. Then, before he closed the starting switch, he drew a pistollike weapon and checked it.

In theory, the Ghaldron-Hesthor paratemporal transposition field was uninfluenced by material objects outside it. In practice, however, such objects occasionally intruded, and sometimes they were alive and hostile. The last time he had been in this conveyer room, he had seen a quartet of returning officers emerge from a conveyer dome dragging a dead lion by the tail. The sigma-ray needler, which he carried, was the only weapon which could be used, under the circumstances. It had no effect whatever on any material structure and could be used inside an activated conveyer without deranging the conductor-mesh, as, say, a bullet or the vibration of an ultrasonic paralyzer would do, and it was instantly fatal to anything having a central nervous system. It was a good weapon to use outtime for that reason, also; even on the most civilized time-line, the most elaborate autopsy would reveal no specific cause of death.

"What's the Esaron Sector like?" Dalla asked, as the conveyer dome around them coruscated with shifting light and vanished.

"Third Level; probability of abortive attempt to colonize this planet from Mars about a hundred thousand years ago," he said. "A few survivors — a shipload or so — were left to shift for themselves while the parent civilization on Mars died out. They lost all vestiges of their original Martian culture, even memory of their extraterrestrial origin. About fifteen hundred to two thousand years ago, a reasonably high electrochemical civilization developed and they began working with nuclear energy and developed reaction-drive spaceships. But they'd concentrated so on the inorganic sciences, and so far neglected the bio-sciences, that when they launched their first ship for Venus they hadn't yet developed a germ theory of disease."

"What happened when they ran into the green-vomit fever?" Dalla asked.

"About what you could expect. The first — and only — ship to return brought it back to Terra. Of course, nobody knew what it was, and before the epidemic ended, it had almost depopulated this planet. Since the survivors knew nothing about germs, they blamed it on the anger of the gods — the old story of recourse to supernaturalism in the absence of a known explanation — and a fanatically anti-scientific cult got control. Of course, space travel was taboo; so was nuclear and even electric power. For some reason, steam power and gunpowder weren't offensive to the gods. They went back to a low-order steam-power, black-powder, culture, and haven't gotten beyond that to this day. The relatively civilized regions are on the east coast of Asia and the west coast of North America; civilized race more or less Caucasian. Political organization just barely above the tribal level — thousands of petty kingdoms and republics and principalities and feudal holdings and robbers' roosts. The principal industries are brigandage, piracy, slave-raiding, cattle-rustling and intercommunal warfare. They have a few ramshackle steam railways, and some steamboats on the rivers. We sell them coal and manufactured goods, mostly in exchange for foodstuffs and tobacco. Consolidated Outtime Foodstuffs has the sector franchise. That's one of the companies Thalvan Dras gets his money from."

They had run down through the civilized Second and Third Levels and were leaving the Fourth behind and entering the Fifth, existing in the probability of a world without human population. Once in a while, around them, they caught brief flashes of buildings and rocketports and spaceports and landing stages, as the conveyer took them through narrow paratime belts on which their own civilization had established outposts — Fifth Level Commercial, Fifth Level Passenger, Industrial Sector, Service Sector.

Finally the conveyer dome around them shimmered into visibility and materialized; when they emerged, there were policemen in green uniforms who entered to search the dome with drawn needlers to make sure they had picked up nothing dangerous on the way. The room outside was similar to the one they had left on Home Time Line, even to the shifting, noisy crowd in incongruously-mixed costumes.

The rocketport was a ten minutes' trip by aircar from the conveyer head; when they boarded the stubby-winged strato-rocket, Vall saw that two of the passenger-seats had square metal cabinets bolted in place behind them and blue plastic helmets on swinging arms mounted above them.

"Everything's set up," the pilot told them. "Dr. Hadron, you sit on the left; that cabinet's loaded with language tape for Acalan. Yours is loaded with a tape of Kharanda; that's the Fourth Level Kholghoor language you wanted, Chief's Assistant. Shall I help you get fixed in your seats?"

"Yes, if you please. Here, Dalla, I'll fix that for you."

Dalla was already asleep when the pilot was adjusting his helmet and giving him his injection. He never felt the rocket tilt into firing position, and while he slept, the Kharands language, with all its vocabulary and grammar, became part of his subconscious knowledge, needing only the mental pronunciation of a trigger-symbol to bring it into consciousness. The pilot was already unfastening and raising his helmet when he opened his eyes. Dalla, beside him, was sipping a cup of spiced wine.

On the landing stage of the Sector-Regional Headquarters at Novilan Equivalent, four or five people were waiting for them. Vall recognized the subchief, Vulthor Tharn, who introduced another man, in riding boots and a white cloak, as Skordran Kirv. Vall clasped hands with him warmly.

"Good work, Agent Skordran. You got onto this promptly."

"I tried to, sir. Do you want the dope now? We have half an hour's flight to our spatial equivalent, and another half hour in transposition."

"Give it to me on the way," he said, and turned to Vulthor Tharn. "Our Esaron costumes ready?"

"Yes. Over there in the control tower. We have a temporary conveyer head set up about two hundred miles south of here, which will take you straight through to the plantation."

"Suppose you change now, Dalla," he said. "Subchief, I'd like a word with you privately."

He and Vulthor Tharn excused themselves and walked over to the edge of the landing stage. The SecReg Subchief was outwardly composed, but Vall sensed that he was worried and embarrassed.

"Now, what's been done since you got Agent Skordran's report?" Vall asked.

"Well, sir, it seems that this is more serious than we had anticipated. Field Agent Skordran, who will give you the particulars, says that there is every indication that a large and well-organized gang of paratemporal criminals, our own people, are at work. He says that he's found evidence of activities on Fourth Level Kholghoor that don't agree with any information we have about conditions on that sector."

"Beside transmitting Agent Skordran's report to Dhergabar through the robot report-system, what have you done about it?"

"I confirmed Agent Skordran in charge of the local investigation, and gave him two detectives and a psychist, sir. As soon as we could furnish hypno-mech indoctrination in Kharanda to other psychists, I sent them along. He now has four of them, and eight detectives. By that time, we had a conveyer head right at this Consolidated Outtime Foodstuffs plantation."

"Why didn't you just borrow psychists from SecReg for Kholghoor, Eastern India?" Vall asked. "Subchief Ranthar would have loaned you a few."

"Oh, I couldn't call on another SecReg for men without higher-echelon authorization. Especially not from another Sector Organization, even another Level Authority," Vulthor Tharn said. "Beside, it would have taken longer to bring them here than hypno-mech our own personnel."

He was right about the second point. Vall agreed mentally; however, his real reason was procedural.

"Did you alert Ranthar Jard to what was going on in his SecReg?" he asked.

"Gracious, no!" Vulthor Tharn was scandalized. "I have no authority to tell people of equal echelon in other Sector and Level organizations what to do. I put my report through regular channels; it wasn't my place to go outside my own jurisdiction."

And his report had crawled through channels for fourteen hours, Vall thought.

"Well, on my authority, and in the name of Chief Tortha, you message Ranthar Jard at once; send him every scrap of information you have on the subject, and forward additional information as it comes in to you. I doubt he'll find anything on any time-line that's being exploited by any legitimate paratimers. This gang probably work exclusively on unpenetrated time-lines; this business Skordran Kirv came across was a bad blunder on some underling's part." He saw Dalla emerge from the control tower in breeches and boots and a white cloak, buckling on a heavy revolver. "I'll go change, now; you get busy calling Ranthar Jard. I'll see you when I get back."

"Are you taking over, Chief's Assistant?" Skordran Kirv asked, as the aircar lifted from the landing stage.

"Not at all. My wife and I are starting on our vacation, as soon as I find out what's been happening here, and report to Chief Tortha. Did your native troopers catch those slavers?"

"Yes, they got them yesterday afternoon; we've had them ever since. Do you want the whole thing just as it happened, Assistant Verkan, or just a condensation?"

"Give me what you think it indicates, remembering that you're probably trying to analyze a large situation from a very small sample."

"It's big, all right," Skordran Kirv said. "This gang can't number less than a hundred men, maybe several hundred. They must have at least two two-hundred-foot conveyers and several small ones, and bases on what sounds like some Fifth Level Time line, and at least one air freighter of around five thousand tons. They are operating on a number of Kholghoor and Esaron time lines."

Verkan Vall nodded. "I didn't think it was any petty larceny," he said.

"Wait till you hear the rest of it. On the Kholghoor Sector, this gang is known as the Wizard Traders; we've been using that as a convenience label. They pose as sorcerers — black robes and hood-masks covered with luminous symbols, voice-amplifiers, cold-light auras, energy-weapons, mechanical magic tricks, that sort of thing. They have all the Croutha scared witless. Their procedure is to establish camps in the forest near recently conquered Kharanda cities; then they appear to the Croutha, impress them with their magical powers, and trade manufactured goods for Kharanda cap-tives. They mainly trade firearms, apparently some kind of flint-locks, and powder."

Then they were confining their operations to unpenetrated time lines; there had been no reports of firearms in the hands of the Croutha invaders.

"After they buy a batch of slaves," Skordran Kirv continued, "they transpose them to this presumably Fifth Level base, where they have concentration camps. The slaves we questioned had been airlifted to North America, where there's another concentration camp, and from there transposed to this Esaron Sector time line where I found them. They say that there were at least two to three thousand slaves in this North American concentration camp and that they are being transposed out in small batches and replaced by others airlifted in from India. This lot was sold to a Calera named Nebu-hin-Abenoz, the chieftain of a hill town, Careba, about fifty miles south-west of the plantation. There were two hundred and fifty in this batch; this Coru-hin-Irigod only bought the batch he sold at the plantation."

The aircar lost speed and altitude; below, the countryside was dotted with conveyer heads, each spatially coexistent with some outtime police post or operation. There were a great many of them; the western coast of North America was a center of civilization on many paratemporal sectors, and while the conveyer heads of the commercial and passenger companies were scattered over hun-dreds of Fifth Level time lines, those of the Paratime Police were concentrated upon one. The anti-grav-car circled around a three-hundred-foot steel tower that supported a conveyer head spatially coexistent with one on a top floor of some outtime tall building, and let down in front of a low prefabricated steel shed. A man in police uniform came out to meet them. There was a fifty-foot conveyer dome inside, and a fifty-foot red-lined circle that marked the transposition point of an outtime conveyer. They all entered the dome, and the operator put on the transposition field.

"You haven't heard the worst of it yet." Skordran Kirv was saying. "On this time line, we have reason to think that the native, Nebu-hin-Abenoz, who bought the slaves, actually saw the slavers' conveyer. Maybe even saw it activated."

"If he did, we'll either have to capture him and give him a memory-obliteration, or kill him," Vall said. "What do you know about him?"

"Well, this Careba, the town he bosses, is a little walled town up in the hills. Everybody there is related to everybody else; this man we have, Coru-hin-Irigod, is the son of a sister of Nebu-hin-Abenoz's wife. They're all bandits and slavers and cattle rustlers and what have you. For the last ten years, Nebu-hin-Abenoz has been buying slaves from some secret source. Before the Kholghoor Sector people began coming in, they were mostly white, with a few brown people who might have been Polynesians. No Negroes — there's no black race on this sector, and I suppose the paratime slavers didn't want too many questions asked. Coru-hin-Irigod, under narco-hypnosis, said that they were all outlanders, speaking strange languages."

"Ten years! And this is the first hint we've had of it," Vall said. "That's not a bright mark for any of us. I'll bet the slave population on some of these Esaron time lines is an anthropologist's nightmare."

"Why, if this has been going on for ten years, there must have been millions upon millions of people dragged from their own time lines into slavery!" Dalla said in a shocked voice.

"Ten years may not be all of it," Vall said. "This Nebu-hin-Abenoz looks like the only tangible lead we have, at present. How does he operate?"

"About once every ten days, he'll take ten or fifteen men and go a day's ride — that may be as much as fifty miles; these Caleras have good horses and they're hard riders — into the hills. He'll take a big bag of money, all gold. After dark, when he has made camp, a couple of strangers in Calera dress will come in. He'll go off with them, and after about an hour, he'll come back with eight or ten of these strangers and a couple of hundred slaves, always chained in batches of ten. Nebu-hin-Abenoz pays for them, makes arrangements for the next meeting, and the next morning he and his party start marching the slaves to Careba. I might add that, until now, these slaves have been sold to the mines east of Careba; these are the first that have gotten into the coastal country."

"That's why this hasn't come to light before, then. The conveyer comes in every ten days, at about the same place?"

"Yes. I've been thinking of a way we might trap them," Skordran Kirv said. "I'll need more men, and equipment."

"Order them from Regional or General Reserve." Vall told him. "This thing's going to have overtop priority till it's cleared up."

He was mentally cursing Vulthor Tharn's procedure-bound timidity as the conveyer flickered and solidified around them and the overhead red light turned green.

They emerged into the interior of a long shed, adobe-walled and thatch-roofed, with small barred windows set high above the earth floor. It was cool and shadowy, and the air was heavy with the fragrance of citrus fruits. There were bins along the walls, some partly full of oranges, and piles of wicker baskets. Another conveyer dome stood beside the one in which they had arrived; two men in white cloaks and riding boots sat on the edge of one of the bins, smoking and talking.

Skordran Kirv introduced them — Gathon Dard and Krador Arv, special detectives — and asked if anything new had come up. Krador Arv shook his head.

"We still have about forty to go," he said. "Nothing new in their stories; still the same two time lines."

"These people," Skordran Kirv explained, "were all peons on the estate of a Kharanda noble just above the big bend of the Ganges. The Croutha hit their master's estate about a ten-days ago, elapsed time. In telling about their capture, most of them say that their master's wife killed herself with a dagger after the Croutha killed her husband, but about one out of ten say that she was kidnaped by the Croutha. Two different time lines, of course. The ones who tell the suicide story saw no firearms among the Croutha; the ones who tell the kidnap story say that they all had some kind of muskets and pistols. We're making synthetic summaries of the two stories."

"We're having trouble with the locals about all these strangers coming in," Gathon Dard added. "They're getting curious."

"We'll have to take a chance on that," Vall said. "Are the interrogations still going on? Then let's have a look-in at them."

The big double doors at the end of the shed were barred on the inside. Krador Arv unlocked a small side door, letting Vall, Dalla and Gathon Dard out. In the yard outside, a gang of slaves were unloading a big wagon of oranges and packing them into hampers; they were guarded by a couple of native riflemen who seemed mostly concerned with keeping them away from the shed, and a man in a white cloak was watching the guards for the same purpose. He walked over and introduced himself to Vall.

"Golzan Doth, local alias Dosu Golan. I'm Consolidated Outtime Foodstuffs' manager here."

"Nasty business for you people," Vall sympathized. "If it's any consolation, it's a bigger headache for us."

"Have you any idea what's going to be done about these slaves?" Golzan Doth asked. "I have to remember that the Company has forty thousand Paratemporal Exchange Units invested in them. The top office was very specific in requesting information about that."

Vall shook his head. "That's over my echelon," he said. "Have to be decided by the Paratime Commission. I doubt if your company'll suffer. You bought them innocently, in conformity with local custom. Ever buy slaves from this Coru-hin-Irigod before?"

"I'm new, here. The man I'm replacing broke his neck when his horse put a foot in a gopher hole about two ten-days ago."

Beside him, Vall could see Dalla nod as though making a mental note. When she got back to Home Time Line, she'd put a crew of mediums to work trying to contact the discarnate former plantation manager; at Rhogom Institute, she had been working on the problem of return of a discarnate personality from outtime.

"A few times," Skordran Kirv said. "Nothing suspicious; all local stuff. We questioned Coru-hin-Irigod pretty closely on that point, and he says that this is the first time he ever brought a batch of Nebu-hin-Abenoz's outlanders this far west."

*   *   *

The interrogations were being conducted inside the plantation house, in the secret central rooms where the paratimers lived. Skordran Kirv used a door-activator to slide open a hidden door.

"I suppose I don't have to warn either of you that any positive statement made in the hearing of a narco-hypnotized subject —" he began.

". . . Has the effect of hypnotic suggestion —" Vall picked up after him.

". . . And should be avoided unless such suggestion is intended," Dalla finished.

Skordran Kirv laughed, opening another, inner door, and stood aside. In what had been the paratimers' recreation room, most of the furniture had been shoved into the corners. Four small tables had been set up, widely spaced and with screens between; across each of them, with an electric recorder between, an almost naked Kharanda slave faced a Paratime Police psychist. At a long table at the far side of the room, four men and two girls were working over stacks of cards and two big charts.

"Phrakor Vuln," the man who was working on the charts introduced himself. "Synthesist." He introduced the others.

Vall made a point of the fact that Dalla was his wife, in case any of the cops began to get ideas, and mentioned that she spoke Kharanda, had spent some time on the Fourth Level Kholghoor, and was a qualified psychist.

"What have you got, so far?" he asked.

"Two different time lines, and two different gangs of Wizard Traders," Phrakor Vuln said. "We've established the latter from physical descriptions and because both batches were sold by the Croutha at equivalent periods of elapsed time."

Vall picked up one of the kidnap-story cards and glanced at it.

"I notice there's a fair verbal description of these firearms, and mention of electric whips," he said. "I'm curious about where they came from."

"Well, this is how we reconstructed them, Chief's Assistant," one of the girls said, handing him a couple of sheets of white drawing paper.

The sketches had been done with soft pencil; they bore repeated erasures and corrections. That of the whip showed a cylindrical handle, indicated as twelve inches in length and one in diameter, fitted with a thumb-switch.

"That's definitely Second Level Khiftan," Vall said, handing it back. "Made of braided copper or silver wire and powered with a little nuclear-conversion battery in the grip. They heat up to about two hundred centigrade; produce really painful burns."

"Why, that's beastly!" Dalla exclaimed.

"Anything on the Khiftan Sector is." Skordran Kirv looked at the four slaves at the tables. "We don't have a really bad case here, now. A few of these people were lash-burned horribly, though."

Vall was looking at the other sketches. One was a musket, with a wide butt and a band-fastened stock; the lock-mechanism, vaguely flintlock, had been dotted in tentatively. The other was a long pistol, similarly definite in outline and vague in mechanical detail; it was merely a knob-butted miniature of the musket.

"I've seen firearms like these; have a lot of them in my collection," he said, handing back the sketches. "Low-order mechanical or high-order pre-mechanical cultures. Fact is, things like those could have been made on the Kholghoor Sector, if the Kharandas had learned to combine sulfur, carbon and nitrates to make powder."

The interrogator at one of the tables had evidently heard all his subject could tell him. He rose, motioning the slave to stand.

"Now, go with that man," he said in Kharanda, motioning to one of the detectives in native guard uniform. "You will trust him; he is your friend and will not harm you. When you have left this room, you will forget everything that has happened here, except that you were kindly treated and that you were given wine to drink and your hurts were anointed. You will tell the others that we are their friends and that they have nothing to fear from us. And you will not try to remove the mark from the back of your left hand."

As the detective led the slave out a door at the other side of the room, the psychist came over to the long table, handing over a card and lighting a cigarette.

"Suicide story," he said to one of the girls, who took the card.

"Anything new?"

"Some minor details about the sale to the Caleras on this time line. I think we've about scraped bottom."

"You can't say that," Phrakor Vuln objected. "The very last one may give us something nobody else had noticed."

Another subject was sent out. The interrogator came over to the table.

"One of the kidnap-story crowd," he said. "This one was right beside that Croutha who took the shot at the wild pig or whatever it was on the way to the Wizard Traders' camp. Best description of the guns we've gotten so far. No question that they're flintlocks." He saw Verkan Vall. "Oh, hello, Assistant Verkan. What do you make of them? You're an authority on outtime weapons, I understand."

"I'd have to see them. These people simply don't think mechanically enough to give a good description. A lot of peoples make flintlock firearms."

He started running over, in his mind, the paratemporal areas in which gunpowder but not the percussion-cap was known. Expanding cultures, which had progressed as far as the former but not the latter. Static cultures, in which an accidental discovery of gunpowder had never been followed up by further research. Post-debacle cultures, in which a few stray bits of ancient knowledge had survived.

Another interrogator came over, and then the fourth. For a while they sat and talked and drank coffee, and then the next quartet of slaves, two men and two women, were brought in. One of the women had been badly blistered by the electric whips of the Wizard Traders; in spite of reassurances, all were visibly apprehensive.

"We will not harm you," one of the psychists told them. "Here; here is medicine for your hurts. At first, it will sting, as good medicines will, but soon it will take away all pain. And here is wine for you to drink."

A couple of detectives approached, making a great show of pouring wine and applying ointment; under cover of the medication, they jabbed each slave with a hypodermic needle, and then guided them to seats at the four tables. Vall and Dalla went over and stood behind one of the psychists, who had a small flashlight in his hand.

"Now, rest for a while," the psychist was saying. "Rest and let the good medicine do its work. You are tired and sleepy. Look at this magic light, which brings comfort to the troubled. Look at the light. Look . . . at . . . the . . . light."

They moved to the next table.

"Did you have hand in the fighting?"

"No, lord. We were peasant folk, not fighting people. We had no weapons, nor weapon-skill. Those who fought were all killed; we held up empty hands, and were spared to be captives of the Croutha."

"What happened to your master, the Lord Ghromdour, and to his lady?"

"One of the Croutha threw a hatchet and killed our master, and then his lady drew a dagger and killed herself."

The psychist made a red mark on the card in front of him, and circled the number on the back of the slave's hand with red indelible crayon. Vall and Dalla went to the third table.

"They had the common weapons of the Croutha, lord, and they also had the weapons of the Wizard Traders. Of these, they carried the long weapons slung across their backs, and the short weapons thrust through their belts."

A blue mark on the card; a blue circle on the back of the slave's hand.

They listened to both versions of what had happened at the sack of the Lord Ghromdour's estate, and the march into the captured city of Jhirda, and the second march into the forest to the camp of the Wizard Traders.

"The servants of the Wizard Traders did not appear until after the Croutha had gone away; they wore different garb. They wore short jackets, and trousers, and short boots, and they carried small weapons on their belts —"

"They had whips of great cruelty that burned like fire; we were all lashed with these whips, as you may see, lord —"

"The Croutha had bound us two and two, with neck-yokes; these the servants of the Wizard Traders took off from us, and they chained us together by tens, with the chains we still wore when we came to this place —"

"They killed my child, my little Zhouzha!" the woman with the horribly blistered back was wailing. "They tore her out of my arms, and one of the servants of the Wizard Traders — may Khokhaat devour his soul forever! — dashed out her brains. And when I struggled to save her. I was thrown on the ground, and beaten with the fire-whips until I fainted. Then I was dragged into the forest, along with the others who were chained with me." She buried her head in her arms, sobbing bitterly.

Dalla stepped forward, taking the flashlight from the interrogator with one hand and lifting the woman's head with the other.

She flashed the light quickly in the woman's eyes.

"You will grieve no more for your child," she said. "Already, you are forgetting what happened at the Wizard Traders' camp, and remembering only that your child is safe from harm. Soon you will remember her only as a dream of the child you hope to have, some day." She flashed the light again, then handed it back to the psychist. "Now, tell us what happened when you were taken into the forest; what did you see there?"

The psychist nodded approvingly, made a note on the card, and listened while the woman spoke. She had stopped sobbing, now, and her voice was clear and cheerful.

Vall went over to the long table.

"Those slaves were still chained with the Wizard Traders' chains when they were delivered here. Where are the chains?" he asked Skordran Kirv.

"In the permanent conveyer room," Skordran Kirv said. "You can look at them there; we didn't want to bring them in here, for fear these poor devils would think we were going to chain them again. They're very light, very strong; some kind of alloy steel. Files and power saws only polish them; it takes fifteen seconds to cut a link with an atomic torch. One long chain, and short lengths, fifteen inches long, staggered, every three feet, with a single hinge-shackle for the ankle. The shackles were riveted with soft wrought-iron rivets, evidently made with some sort of a power riveting-machine. We cut them easily with a cold chisel."

"They ought to be sent to Dhergabar Equivalent, Police Terminal, for study of material and workmanship. Now, you mentioned some scheme you had for capturing this conveyer that brings in the slaves for Nebu-hin-Abenoz. What have you in mind?"

"We still have Coru-hin-Irigod and all his gang, under hypno. I'd thought of giving them hypnotic conditioning, and sending them back to Careba with orders to put out some kind of signal the next time Nebu-hin-Abenoz starts out on a buying trip. We could have a couple of men posted in the hills overlooking Careba, and they could send a message-ball through to Police Terminal. Then, a party could be sent with a mobile conveyer to ambush Nebu-hin-Abenoz on the way, and wipe out his party. Our people could take their horses and clothing and go on to take the conveyer by surprise."

"I'd suggest one change. Instead of relying on visual signals by the hypno-conditioned Coru-hin-Irigod, send a couple of our men to

Careba with midget radios."

Skordran Kirv nodded. "Sure. We can condition Coru-hin-Irigod to accept them as friends and vouch for them at Careba. Our boys can be traders and slave buyers. Careba's a market town; traders are always welcome. They can have firearms to sell — revolvers and repeating rifles. Any Calera'll buy any firearm that's better than the one he's carrying; they'll always buy revolvers and repeaters. We can get what we want from Commercial Four-Oh-Seven; we can get riding and pack horses here."

Vall nodded. "And the post overlooking or in radio range of Careba on this time line, and another on PolTerm. For the ambush of Nebu-hin-Abenoz's gang and the capture of the conveyer, use anything you want to — sleep-gas, paralyzers, energy-weapons, antigrav-equipment, anything. As far as regulations about using only equipment appropriate to local culture-levels, forget them entirely. But take that conveyer intact. You can locate the base time line from the settings of the instrument panel, and that's what we want most of all."

Dalla and the police psychist, having finished with and dismissed their subject, came over to the long table.

". . . That poor creature," Dalla was saying. "What sort of fiends are they?"

"If that made you sick, remember we've been listening to things like that for the last eight hours. Some of the stories were even worse than that one."

"Well, I'd like to use a heat-gun on the whole lot of them, turned down to where it'd just fry them medium-rare," Dalla said. "And for whoever's back of this, take him to Second Level Khiftan and sell him to the priests of Fasif."

"Too bad you're not coming back from your vacation, instead of starting out, Chief's Assistant Verkan," Skordran Kirv said. "This is too big for me to handle alone, and I'd sooner work under you than anybody else Chief Tortha sends in."

"Vall!" Dalla cried in indignation. "You're not going to just report on this and then walk away from it, are you?"

"But, darling," Vall replied, in what he hoped was a convincing show of surprise. "You don't want our vacation postponed again, do you? If I get mixed up in this, there's no telling when I can get away, and by the time I'm free, something may come up at Rhogom Institute that you won't want to drop —"

"Vall, you know perfectly well that I wouldn't be happy for an instant on the Dwarma Sector, thinking about this —"

"All right, then; let's forget about the vacation. You want to stay on for a while and help me with this? It'll be a lot of hard work, but we'll be together."

"Yes, of course. I want to do something to smash those devils. Vall, if you'd heard some of the things they did to those poor people —"

"Well, I'll have to go back to PolTerm, as soon as I'm reasonably well filled in on this, and report to Tortha Karf and tell him I've taken charge. You can stay here and help with these interrogations; I'll be back in about ten hours. Then, we can go to Kholghoor East India SecReg HQ to talk to Ranthar Jard. We may be able to get something that'll help us on that end —"

"You may be able to have your vacation before too long, Dr. Hadron," Skordran Kirv told her. "Once we capture one of their conveyers, the instrument panel'll tell us what time line they're working from, and then we'll have them."

"There's an Indo-Turanian Sector parable about a snake charmer who thought he was picking up his snake and found that he had hold of an elephant's tail," Vall said. "That might be a good thing to bear in mind, till we find out just what we have picked up."

Coming down a hallway on the hundred and seventh floor of the Management wing of the Paratime Building, Yandar Yadd paused to admire, in the green mirror of the glassoid wall, the jaunty angle of his silver-feathered cap, the fit of his short jacket, and the way his weapon hung at his side. This last was not instantly recognizable as a weapon; it looked more like a portable radio, which indeed it was. It was, none the less, a potent weapon. One flick of his finger could connect that radio with one at Tri-Planet News Service, and within the hour anything he said into it would be heard by all Terra, Mars and Venus. In consequence, there existed around the Paratime Building a marked and understandable reluctance to antagonize Yandar Yadd.

He glanced at his watch. It was twenty minutes short of 1000, when he had an appointment with Baltan Vrath, the comptroller general. Glancing about, he saw that he was directly in front of the doorway of the Outtime Claims Bureau, and he strolled in, walking through the waiting room and into the claims-presentation office. At once, he stiffened like a bird dog at point.

Sphabron Larv, one of his young legmen, was in altercation across the counter-desk with Varkar Klav, the Deputy Claims Agent on duty at the time. Varkar was trying to be icily dignified; Sphabron Larv's black hair was in disarray and his face was suffused with anger. He was pounding with his fist on the plastic counter-top.

"You have to!" he was yelling in the older man's face. "That's a public document, and I have a right to see it. You want me to go into Tribunes' Court and get an order? If I do, there'll be a Question in Council about why I had to, before the day's out!"

"What's the matter, Larv?" Yandar Yadd asked lazily. "He trying to hold something out on you?"

Sphabron Larv turned; his eyes lit happily when he saw his boss, and then his anger returned.

"I want to see a copy of an indemnity claim that was filed this morning," he said. "Varkar, here, won't show it to me. What does he think this is, a Fourth Level dictatorship?"

"What kind of a claim, now?" Yandar Yadd addressed Larv, ignoring Varkar Klav.

"Consolidated Outtime Foodstuffs — one of the Thalvan Interests companies — just claimed forty thousand P.E.U. for a hundred slaves bought by one of their plantation managers on Third Level Esaron from a local slave dealer. The Paratime Police impounded the slaves for narco-hypnotic interrogation, and then transposed the lot of them to Police Terminal."

Yandar Yadd still held his affectation of sleepy indolence.

"Now why would the Paracops do that, I wonder? Slavery's an established local practice on Esaron Sector; our people have to buy slaves if they want to run a plantation."

"I know that." Sphabron Larv replied. "That's what I want to find out. There must be something wrong, either with the slaves, or the treatment our people were giving them, or the Paratime Police, and I want to find out which."

"To tell the truth, Larv, so do I." Yandar Yadd said. He turned to the man behind the counter. "Varkar, do we see that claim, or do I make a story out of your refusal to show it?" he asked.

"The Paratime Police asked me to keep this confidential," Varkar Klav said. "Publicity would seriously hamper an important police investigation."

Yandar Yadd made an impolite noise. "How do I know that all it would do would be to reveal police incompetence?" he retorted. "Look, Varkar; you and the Paratime Police and the Paratime Commission and the Home Time Line Management are all hired employees of the Home Time Line public. The public has a right to know what its employees are doing, and it's my business to see that they're informed. Now, for the last time — will you show us a copy of that claim?"

"Well, let me explain, off the record —" the official begged.

"Huh-uh! Huh-uh! I had that off-the-record gag worked on me when I was about Larv's age, fifty years ago. Anything I get, I put on the air or not at my own discretion."

"All right," Varkar Klav surrendered, pointing to a reading screen and twiddling a knob. "But when you read it, I hope you have enough discretion to keep quiet about it."

The screen lit, and Yandar Yadd automatically pressed a button for a photo-copy. The two newsmen stared for a moment, and then even Yandar Yadd's shell of drowsy negligence cracked and fell from him. His hand brushed the switch as he snatched the hand-phone from his belt.

"Marva!" he barked, before the girl at the news office could more than acknowledge. "Get this recorded for immediate telecast! . . . Ready? Beginning: The existence of a huge paratemporal slave trade came to light on the afternoon of One-Five-Nine Day, on a time line of the Third Level Esaron Sector, when Field Agent Skordran Kirv, Paratime Police, discovered, at an orange plantation of Consolidated Outtime Foodstuffs —"

Salgath Trod sat alone in his private office, his half-finished lunch growing cold on the desk in front of him as he watched the teleview screen across the room, tuned to a pickup behind the Speaker's chair in the Executive Council Chamber ten stories below. The two thousand seats had been almost all empty at 1000, when Council had convened. Fifteen minutes later, the news had broken; now, at 1430, a good three quarters of the seats were occupied. He could see, in the aisles, the gold-plated robot pages gliding back and forth, receiving and delivering messages. One had just slid up to the seat of Councilman Hasthor Flan, and Hasthor was speaking urgently into the recorder mouthpiece. Another message for him, he supposed; he'd gotten at least a score such calls since the crisis had developed.

People were going to start wondering, he thought. This situation should have been perfect for his purposes; as leader of the Opposition he could easily make himself the next General Manager, if he exploited this scandal properly. He listened for a while to the Centrist-Management member who was speaking; he could rip that fellow's arguments to shreds in a hundred words — but he didn't dare. The Management was taking exactly the line Salgath Trod wanted the whole Council to take: treat this affair as an isolated and extraordinary occurrence, find a couple of convenient scapegoats, cobble up some explanation acceptable to the public, and forget it. He wondered what had happened to the imbecile who had transposed those Kholghoor Sector slaves onto an exploited time line. Ought to be shanghaied to the Khiftan Sector and sold to the priests of Fasif!

A buzzer sounded, and for an instant he thought it would be the message he had seen Hasthor Fan recording. Then he realized that it was the buzzer for the private door, which could only be operated by someone with a special identity sign. He pressed a button and unlocked the door.

The young man in the loose wrap-around tunic who entered was a stranger. At least, his face and his voice were strange, but voices could be mechanically altered, and a skilled cosmetician could render any face unrecognizable. He looked like a student, or a minor commercial executive, or an engineer, or something like that. Of course, his tunic bulged slightly under the left armpit, but even the most respectable tunics showed occasional weapon-bulges.

"Good afternoon, councilman," the newcomer said, sitting down across the desk from Salgath Trod. "I was just talking to . . . somebody we both know."

Salgath Trod offered cigarettes, lighted his visitor's and then his own.

"What does Our Mutual Friend think about all this?" he asked, gesturing toward the screen.

"Our Mutual Friend isn't at all happy about it."

"You think, perhaps, that I'm bursting into wild huzzas?" Salgath Trod asked. "If I were to act as everybody expects me to, I'd be down there on the floor, now, clawing into the Management tooth and nail. All my adherents are wondering why I'm not. So are all my opponents, and before long one of them is going to guess the reason."

"Well, why not go down?" the stranger asked. "Our Mutual Friend thinks it would be an excellent idea. The leak couldn't be stopped, and it's gone so far already that the Management will never be able to play it down. So the next best thing is to try to exploit it."

Salgath Trod smiled mirthlessly. "So I am to get in front of it, and lead it in the right direction? Fine . . . as long as I don't stumble over something. If I do, it'll go over me like a Fifth Level bison-herd."

"Don't worry about that," the stranger laughed reassuringly. "There are others on the floor who are also friends of Our Mutual Friend. Here: what you'd better do is attack the Paratime Police, especially Tortha Karf and Verkan Vall. Accuse them of negligence and incompetence, and, by implication, of collusion, and demand a special committee to investigate. And try to get a motion for a confidence vote passed. A motion to censure the Management, say —"

Salgath Trod nodded. "It would delay things, at least. And if Our Mutual Friend can keep properly covered, I might be able to overturn the Management." He looked at the screen again. "That old fool of a Nanthav is just getting started; it'll be an hour before I could get recognized. Plenty of time to get a speech together. Something short and vicious —"

"You'll have to be careful. It won't do, with your political record, to try to play down these stories of a gigantic criminal conspiracy. That's too close to the Management line. And at the same time, you want to avoid saying anything that would get Verkan Vall and Tortha Karf started off on any new lines of investigation."

Salgath Trod nodded. "Just depend on me; I'll handle it."

After the stranger had gone, he shut off the sound reception, relying on visual dumb-show to keep him informed of what was going on on the Council floor. He didn't like the situation. It was too easy to say the wrong thing. If only he knew more about the shadowy figures whose messengers used his private door —

Coru-hin-Irigod held his aching head in both hands, as though he were afraid it would fall apart, and blinked in the sunlight from the window. Lord Safar, how much of that sweet brandy had he drunk, last night? He sat on the edge of the bed for a moment, trying to think. Then, suddenly apprehensive, he thrust his hand under his pillow. The heavy four-barreled pistols were there, all right, but — *The money*!

He rummaged frantically among the bedding, and among his clothes, piled on the floor, but the leather bag was nowhere to be found. Two thousand gold *obus*, the price of a hundred slaves. He snatched up one of the pistols, his headache forgotten. Then he laughed and tossed the pistol down again. Of course! He'd given the bag to the plantation manager, what was his outlandish name, Dosu Golan, to keep for him before the drinking bout had begun. It was safely waiting for him in the plantation strong box. Well, nothing like a good scare to make a man forget a brandy head, anyhow. And there was something else, something very nice —

Oh, yes, there it was, beside the bed. He picked up the beautiful gleaming repeater, pulled down the lever far enough to draw the cartridge halfway out of the chamber, and closed it again, lowering the hammer. Those two Jeseru traders from the North, what were their names? Ganadara and Atarazola. That was a stroke of luck, meeting them here. They'd given him this lovely rifle, and they were going to accompany him and his men back to Careba; they had a hundred such rifles, and two hundred six-shot revolvers, and they wanted to trade for slaves. The Lord Safar bless them both, wouldn't they be welcome at Careba!

He looked at the sunlight falling through the window on the still recumbent form of his companion, Faru-hin-Obaran. Outside, he could hear the sounds of the plantation coming to life — an ax thudding on wood, the clatter of pans from the kitchens. Crossing to Faru-hin-Obaran's bed, he grasped the sleeper by the ankle, tugging.

"Waken, Faru!" he shouted. "Get up and clear the fumes from your head! We start back to Careba today!"

Faru swore groggily and pushed himself into a sitting position, fumbling on the floor for his trousers.

"What day's this?" he asked.

"The day after we went to bed, ninny!" Then Coru-hin-Irigod wrinkled his brow. He could remember, clearly enough, the sale of the slaves, but after that — Oh, well, he'd been drinking; it would all come back to him, after a while.

*　　　*　　　*

Verkan Vall rubbed his hand over his face wearily, started to light another cigarette, and threw it across the room in disgust. What he needed was a drink — a long drink of cool, tart white wine, laced with brandy — and then he needed to sleep.

"We're absolutely nowhere!" Ranthar Jard said. "Of course they're operating on time lines we've never penetrated. The fact that they're supplying the Croutha with guns proves that; there isn't a firearm on any of the time lines our people are legitimately exploiting. And there are only about three billion time lines on this belt of the Croutha invasion —"

"If we could think of a way to reduce it to some specific area of paratime —" one of Ranthar Jard's deputies began.

"That's precisely what we've been trying to do, Klav," Vall said. "We haven't done it."

Dalla, who had withdrawn from the discussion and was on a couch at the side of the room, surrounded by reports and abstracts and summaries, looked up.

"I took hours and hours of hypno-mech on Kholghoor Sector religions, before I went out on that wild-goose chase for psychokinesis and precognition data," she said. "About six or eight hundred years ago, there were religious wars and heresies and religious schisms all over the Kharanda country. No matter how uniform the Kholghoor Sector may be otherwise, there are dozens and dozens of small belts and sub-sectors of different religions or sects or god-cults."

"That's right," Ranthar Jard agreed, brightening. "We have hagiologists who know all that stuff; we'll have a couple of them interrogate those slaves. I don't know how much they can get out of them — lot of peasants, won't be up on the theological niceties — but a synthesis of what we get from the lot of them —"

"That's an idea," Vall agreed. "About the first idea we've had, here — Oh, how about politics, too? Check on who's the king, what the stories about the royal family are, that sort of thing."

Ranthar Jard looked at the map on the wall. "The Croutha have only gotten halfway to Nharkan, here. Say we transpose detectives in at night on some of these time lines we think are promising, and check up at the tax-collection offices on a big landowner north of Jhirda named Ghromdour? That might get us something."

"Well, I don't want you to think we're trying to get out of work, Chief's Assistant," one of the deputies said, "but is there any real necessity for our trying to locate the Wizard Trader time lines? If you can get them from the Esaron Sector, it'll be the same, won't it?"

"Marv, in this business you never depend on just one lead," Ranthar Jard told him. "And beside, when Skordran Kirv's gang hits the base of operations in North America, there's no guarantee that they may not have time to send off a radio warning to the crowd at the base here in India. We have to hit both places at once."

"Well, that, too," Vall said. "But the main thing is to get these Wizard Trader camps on the Kholghoor Sector cleaned out. How are you fixed for men and equipment, for a big raid, Jard?"

Ranthar Jard shrugged. "I can get about five hundred men with conveyers, including a couple of two-hundred-footers to carry airboats," he said.

"Not enough. Skordran Kirv has one complete armored brigade, one airborne infantry brigade, and an air cavalry regiment, with Ghaldron-Hesthor equipment for a simultaneous transposition," Vall said.

"Where in blazes did he get them all?" Ranthar Jard demanded.

"They're guard troops, from Service Sector and Industrial Sector. We'll get you the same sort of a force. I only hope we don't have another Prole insurrection while they're away —"

"Well, don't think I'm trying to argue policy with you," Ranthar Jard said, "but that could raise a dreadful stink on Home Time Line. Especially on top of this news-break about the slave trade."

"We'll have to take a chance on that," Vall said. "If you're worried about what the book says, forget it. We're throwing the book away, on this operation. Do you realize that this thing is a threat to the whole Paratime Civilization?"

"Of course I do," Ranthar Jard said. "I know the doctrine of Paratime Security as well as you or anybody else. The question is, does the public realize it?"

A buzzer sounded. Ranthar Jard pressed a switch on the intercom-box in front of him and said: "Ranthar here. Well?"

"Visiphone call, top urgency, just came in for Chief's Assistant Verkan, from Novilan Equivalent. Where can I put it through, sir?"

"Here; booth seven." Ranthar Jard pointed across the room, nodding to Vall. "In just a moment."

Gathon Dard and Antrath Alv — temporary local aliases, Ganadara and Atarazola — sat relaxed in their saddles, swaying to the motion of their horses. They wore the rust-brown hooded cloaks of the northern Jeseru people, in sober contrast to the red and yellow and blue striped robes and sun-bonnets of the Caleras in whose company they rode. They carried short repeating carbines in saddle scabbards, and heavy revolvers and long knives on their belts, and each led six heavily-laden pack-horses.

Coru-hin-Irigod, riding beside Ganadara, pointed up the trail ahead.

"From up there," he said, speaking in Acalan, the lingua franca of the North American West Coast on that sector, "we can see across the valley to Careba. It will be an hour, as we ride, with the pack-horses. Then we will rest, and drink wine, and feast."

Ganadara nodded. "It was the guidance of our gods — and yours, Coru-hin-Irigod — that we met. Such slaves as you sold at the outlanders' plantation would bring a fine price in the North. The men are strong, and have the look of good field-workers; the women are comely and well-formed. Though I fear that my wife would little relish it did I bring home such handmaidens."

Coru-hin-Irigod laughed. "For your wife, I will give you one of our riding whips." He leaned to the side, slashing at a cactus with his quirt. "We in Careba have no trouble with our wives, about handmaidens or anything else."

"By Safar, if you doubt your welcome at Careba, wait till you show your wares," another Calera said. "Rifles and revolvers like those come to our country seldom, and then old and battered, sold or stolen many times before we see them. Rifles that fire seven times without taking butt from shoulder!" He invoked the name of the Great Lord Safar again.

The trail widened and leveled; they all came up abreast, with the pack-horses strung out behind, and sat looking across the valley to the adobe walls of the town that perched on the opposite ridge. After a while, riders began dismounting and checking and tightening saddle-girths; a couple of Caleras helped Ganadara and Atarazola inspect their pack-horses. When they remounted, Atarazola bowed his head, lifting his left sleeve to cover his mouth, and muttered into it at some length. The Caleras looked at him curiously, and Coru-hin-Irigod inquired of Ganadara what he did.

"He prays," Ganadara said. "He thanks our gods that we have lived to see your town, and asks that we be spared to bring many more trains of rifles and ammunition up this trail."

The slaver nodded understandingly. The Caleras were a pious people, too, who believed in keeping on friendly terms with the gods.

"May Safar's hand work with the hands of your gods for it," he said, making what, to a non-Calera, would have been an extremely ribald sign.

"The gods watch over us," Atarazola said, lifting his head. "They are near us even now; they have spoken words of comfort in my ear.'"

Ganadara nodded. The gods to whom his partner prayed were a couple of paratime policemen, crouching over a radio a mile or so down the ridge.

"My brother," he told Coru-hin-Irigod, "is much favored by our gods. Many people come to him to pray for them."

"Yes. So you told me, now that I think on it." That detail had been included in the pseudo-memories he had been given under hypnosis. "I serve Safar, as do all Caleras, but I have heard that the Jeserus' gods are good gods, dealing honestly with their servants."

An hour later, under the walls of the town, Coru-hin-Irigod drew one of his pistols and fired all four barrels in rapid succession into the air, shouting, "Open! Open for Coru-hin-Irigod, and for the Jeseru traders, Ganadara and Atarazola, who are with him!"

A head, black-bearded and sun-bonneted, appeared between the brick merlons of the wall above the gate, shouted down a welcome, and then turned away to bawl orders. The gate slid aside, and, after the caravan had passed through, naked slaves pushed the massive thing shut again. Although they were familiar with the interior of the town, from photographs taken with boomerang-balls — automatic-return transposition spheres like message-balls — they looked around curiously. The central square was thronged — Caleras in striped robes, people from the south and east in baggy trousers and embroidered shirts, mountaineers in deerskins. A slave market was in progress, and some hundred-odd items of human merchandise were assembled in little groups, guarded by their owners and inspected by prospective buyers. They seemed to be all natives of that geographic and paratemporal area.

"Don't even look at those," Coru-hin-Irigod advised. "They are but culls; the market is almost over. We'll go to the house of Nebu-hin-Abenoz, where all the considerable men gather, and you will find those who will be able to trade slaves worthy of the goods you have with you. Meanwhile, let my people take your horses and packs to my house; you shall be my guests while you stay in Careba."

It was perfectly safe to trust Coru-hin-Irigod. He was a murderer and a brigand and a slaver, but he would never incur the scorn of men and the curse of the gods by dealing foully with a guest. The horses and packs were led away by his retainers; Gana-dara and Atarazola pushed their horses after his and Faru-hin-Obaran's through the crowd.

The house of Nebu-hin-Abenoz, like every other building in Careba, was flat-roofed, adobe-walled and window-less except for narrow rifle-slits. The wide double-gate stood open, and five or six heavily armed Caleras lounged just inside. They greeted Coru and Faru by name, and the strangers by their assumed nationality. The four rode through, into what appeared to be the stables, turning their horses over to slaves, who took them away. There were between fifty and sixty other horses in the place.

Divesting themselves of their weapons in an anteroom at the head of a flight of steps, they passed under an arch and into a wide, shady patio, where thirty or forty men stood about or squatted on piles of cushions, smoking cheroots, drinking from silver cups, talking in a continuous babel. Most of them were in Calera dress, though there were men of other communities and nations, in other garb. As they moved across the patio, Gathon Dard caught snatches of conversations about deals in slaves, and horse trades, about bandit raids and blood feuds, about women and horses and weapons.

An old man with a white beard and an unusually clean robe came over to intercept them.

"Ha, lord of my daughter, you're back at last. We had begun to fear for you," he said.

"Nothing to fear, father of my wife," Coru-hin-Irigod replied. "We sold the slaves for a good price, and tarried the night feasting in good company. Such good company that we brought some of it with us — Atarazola and Ganadara, men of the Jeseru; Cavu-hin-Avoran, whose daughter mothered my sons." He took his father-in-law by the sleeve and pulled him aside, motioning Gathon Dard and Antrath Alv to follow.

"They brought weapons; they want outland slaves, of the sort I took to sell in the Big Valley country," he whispered. "The weapons are repeating rifles from across the ocean, and six-shot revolvers. They also have much ammunition."

"Oh, Safar bless you!" the white-beard cried, his eyes brightening. "Name your own price; satisfy yourselves that we have dealt fairly with you; go, and return often again! Come, lord of my daughter; let us make them known to Nebu-hin-Abenoz. But not a word about the kind of weapons you have, strangers, until we can speak privately. Say only that you have rifles to trade."

Gathon Dard nodded. Evidently there was some sort of power-struggle going on in Careba; Coru-hin-Irigod and his wife's father were of the party of Nebu-hin-Abenoz, and wanted the repeaters and six-shooters for themselves.

Nebu-hin-Abenoz, swarthy, hook-nosed, with a square-cut graying beard, lounged in a low chair across the patio; near him four or five other Caleras sat or squatted or reclined, all smoking the rank black tobacco of the country and drinking wine or brandy. Their conversation ceased as Cavu-hin-Avoran and the others approached. The chief of Careba listened to the introduction, then heaved himself to his feet and clapped the newcomers on the shoulders.

"Good, good!" he said. "We know you Jeseru people; you're honest traders. You come this far into our mountains too seldom. We can trade with you. We need weapons. As for the sort of slaves you want, we have none too many now, but in eight days we will have plenty. If you stay with us that long —"

"Careba is a pleasant place to be," Ganadara said. "We can wait."

"What sort of weapons have you?" the chief asked.

"Pistols and rifles, lord of my father's sister," Coru-hin-Irigod answered for them. "The packs have been taken to my house, where our friends will stay. We can bring a few to show you, the hour after evening prayers."

Nebu-hin-Abenoz shot a keen glance at his brother-in-law's son and nodded. "Or, better, I will come to your house then; thus I can see the whole load. How will that be?"

"Better; I will be there, too," Cavu-hin-Avoran said, then turned to Gathon Dard and Antrath Alv. "You have been long on the road; come, let us drink cool wine, and then we will eat," he said. "Until this evening, Nebu-hin-Abenoz."

He led his son-in-law and the traders to one side, where several kegs stood on trestles with cups and flagons beside them. They filled a flagon, took a cup apiece, and went over to a pile of cushions at one side.

As they did, three men came pushing through the crowd toward Nebu-hin-Abenoz's seat. They wore a costume unfamiliar to Gathon Dard — little round caps with red and green streamers behind, and long, wide-sleeved white gowns — and one of them had gold rings in his ears.

"Nebu-hin-Abenoz?" one of them said, bowing. "We are three men of the Usasu cities. We have gold *obus* to spend; we seek a beautiful girl, to be first concubine to our king's son, who is now come to the estate of manhood."

Nebu-hin-Abenoz picked up the silver-mounted pipe he had laid aside, and re-lighted it, frowning.

"Men of the Usasu, you have a heavy responsibility," he said. "You have the responsibility for the future of your kingdom, for a boy's character is more shaped by his first concubine than by his teachers. How old is the boy?"

"Sixteen, Nebu-hin-Abenoz; the age of manhood among us."

"Then you want a girl older, but not much older. She should be versed in the arts of love, but innocent of heart. She should be wise, but teachable; gentle and loving, but with a will of her own —"

The three men in white gowns were fidgeting. Then, suddenly, like three marionettes on a single string, they put their right hands to their mouths and then plunged them into the left sleeves of their gowns, whipping out knives and then sprang as one upon Nebu-hin-Abenoz, slashing and stabbing.

Gathon Dard was on his feet at once; he hurled the wine flagon at the three murderers and leaped across the room. Antrath Alv went bounding after him, and by this time three or four of the group around Nebu-hin-Abenoz's chair had recovered their wits and jumped to their feet. One of the three assailants turned and slashed with his knife, almost disemboweling a Calera who had tried to grapple with him. Before he could free the blade, another Calera brought a brandy bottle down on his head. Gathon Dard sprang upon the back of a second assassin, hooking his left elbow under the fellow's chin and grabbing the wrist of his knife-hand with his right; the man struggled for an instant, then went limp and fell forward. The third of the trio of murderers was still slashing at the fallen chieftain when Antrath Alv chopped him along the side of the neck with the edge of his hand; he simply dropped and lay still.

Nebu-hin-Abenoz was dead. He had been slashed and cut and stabbed in twenty places; his throat had been cut at least three times, and he had almost been decapitated. The wounded Calera wasn't dead yet; however, even if he had been at the moment on the operating table of a First Level Home Time Line hospital, it was doubtful if he could have been saved, and under the circumstances, his life-expectancy could be measured in seconds. Some cushions were placed under his head, and women called to attend him, but he died before they arrived.

The three assassins were also dead. Except for a few cuts on the scalp of the one who had been felled with the bottle, there was not a mark on any of them. Cavu-hin-Avoran kicked one of them in the face and cursed.

"We killed the skunks too quickly!" he cried. "We should have overcome them alive, and then taken our time about dealing with them as they deserved." He went on to specify the nature of their deserts. "Such infamy!"

"Well, I'll swear I didn't think a little tap like I gave that one would kill him," the bottle-wielder excused himself. "Of course, I was thinking only of Nebu-hin-Abenoz, Safar receive him —"

Antrath Alv bent over the one he had hand-chopped.

"I didn't kill this one," he said. "The way I hit him, if I had, his neck would be broken, and it's not. See?" He twisted at the dead man's neck. "I think they took poison before they drew their knives."

"I saw all of them put their hands to their mouths!" a Calera exclaimed. "And look; see how their jaws are clenched." He picked up one of the knives and used it to pry the dead man's jaws apart, sniffing at his lips and looking into his mouth. "Look, his teeth and his tongue are discolored; there is a strange smell, too."

Antrath Alv sniffed, then turned to his partner. "Halatane," he whispered. Gathon Dard nodded. That was a First Level poison; paratimers often carried halatane capsules on the more barbaric time-lines, as a last insurance against torture.

"But, Holy Name of Safar, what manner of men were these?" Coru-hin-Irigod demanded. "There are those I would risk my life to kill, but I would not throw it away thus."

"They came knowing that we would kill them, and took the poison that they might die quickly and without pain," a Calera said.

"Or that your tortures would not wring from them the names and nation of those who sent them," an elderly man in the dress of a rancher from the southeast added. "If I were you, I would try to find out who these enemies are, and the sooner the better."

Gathon Dard was examining one of the knives — a folding knife with a broad single-edged blade, locked open with a spring; the handle was of tortoise shell, bolstered with brass.

"In all my travels," he said, "I never saw a knife of this workmanship before. Tell me, Coru-hin-Irigod, do you know from what country these outland slaves of Nebu-hin-Abenoz's come?"

"You think that might have something to do with it?" the Calera asked.

"It could. I think that these people might not have been born slaves, but people taken captive. Suppose, at some time, there had been sold to Nebu-hin-Abenoz, and sold elsewhere by him, one who was a person of consequence — the son of a king, or the priest of some god," Gathon Dard suggested.

"By Safar, yes! And now that nation, wherever it is, is at blood-feud with us," Cavu-hin-Avoran said. "This must be thought about; it is an ill thing to have unknown enemies."

"Look!" a Calera who had begun to strip the three dead men cried. "These are not of the Usasu cities, or any other people of this land. See, they are uncircumcised!"

"Many of the slaves whom Nebu-hin-Abenoz brought to Careba from the hills have been uncircumcised," Coru-hin-Irigod said. "Jeseru, I think you have your sights on the heart of it." He frowned. "Now, think you, will those who had this done be satisfied, or will they carry on their hatred against all of us?"

"A hard question," Antrath Alv said. "You Caleras do not serve our gods, but you are our friends. Suffer me to go apart and pray; I would take counsel with the gods, that they may aid us all in this."

PART 2

It was full daylight, but the sun was hidden; a thin rain fell on the landing around at Police Terminal Dhergabar Equivalent when Vall and Dalla left the rocket. Across the black lavalike pavement, they could see the bulky form of Tortha Karf, hunched under a long cloak, with his flat cap pulled down over his brow. He shook hands with Vall and kissed cheeks with Dalla when they joined him.

"Car's over here," he said, nodding toward the waiting vehicle. "Yesterday wasn't one of our better days, was it?"

"No. It wasn't." Vall agreed. They climbed into the car, and the driver lifted straight up to two thousand feet and turned, soaring down to land on the Chief's Headquarters Building, a mile away. "We're not completely stopped, sir. Ranthar Jard is working on a few ideas that may lead him to the Kholghoor time lines where the Wizard Traders are operating. If we can't get them through their output, we may nail them at the intake."

"Unless they've gotten the wind up and closed down all their operations," Tortha Karf said.

"I doubt if they've done that, Chief," Vall replied. "We don't know who these people are, of course, and it's hard to judge their reactions, but they're willing to take chances for big gains. I believe they think they're safe, now that they've closed out the compromised time line and killed the only witness against them."

"Well, what's Ranthar Jard doing?"

"Trying to locate the sub-sector and probability belt from what the slaves can tell him about their religious beliefs, about the local king, and the prince of Jhirda, and the noble families of the neighborhood," Vall said. "When he has it localized as closely as he can, he's going to start pelting the whole paratemporal area with photographic auto-return balls dropped from aircars on Police Terminal over the spatial equivalents of a couple of Croutha-conquered cities. As soon as he gets a photo that shows Croutha with firearms, he'll have a Wizard Trader time line."

"Sounds simple," the Chief said. The car landed, and he helped Dalla out. "I suppose both you and he know how many chances against one he has of finding anything." They went over to an antigrav-shaft and floated down to the floor on which Tortha Karf had a duplicate of the office in the Paratime Building on Home Time Line. "It's the only chance we have, though."

"There's one thing that bothers me," Dalla said, as they entered the office and went back behind the horseshoe-shaped desk. "I understand that the news about this didn't break on Home Time Line till the late morning of One-Six-One Day. Nebu-hin-Abenoz was murdered at about 1700 local time, which would be 0100 this morning Dhergabar time. That would give this gang fourteen hours to hear the news, transmit it to their base, and get these three men hypno-conditioned, disguised, transposed to this Esaron Sector time line, and into Careba." She shook her head. "That's pretty fast work."

Tortha Karf looked sidewise at Verkan Vall. "Your girl has the makings of a cop, Vall," he commented.

"She's been a big help, on Esaron and Kholghoor Sectors," Vall said. "She wants to stay with it and help me; I'll be very glad to have her with me."

Tortha Karf nodded. He knew, too, that Dalla wouldn't want to have to go back to Home Time Line and wait the long investigation out.

"Of course; we can use all the help we can get. I think we can get a lot from Dalla. Fix her up with some kind of a title and police status — technical-expert, assistant, or something like that." He clasped hands, man-fashion, with her. "Glad to have you on the cops with us, Dalla," he said. Then he turned to Vall. "There was almost twenty-four hours between the time I heard about this and when this blasted Yandar Yadd got hold of the story. Of all the infernal, irresponsible —" He almost choked with indignation. "And it was another fourteen hours between the time Skordran sent in his report and I heard about it."

"Golzan Doth sent in a report to his company about the same time Skordran Kirv made his first report to his Sector-Regional Subchief." Vall mentioned.

"That might be it," Tortha Karf considered. "I wish there were another explanation, because that implies a very extensive intelligence network, which means a big organization. But I'm afraid that's it. I wish I could pull in everybody in Consolidated Outtime Foodstuffs who handled that report, and narco-hypnotize them. Of course, we can't do things like that on Home Time Line, and with the political situation what it is now —"

"Why, what's been happening, Chief?"

Tortha Karf swore with weary bitterness. "Salgath Trod's what's been happening. At first, after Yandar Yadd broke the story on the air, there was just a lot of unorganized Opposition sniping in Council; Salgath waited till the middle of the afternoon, when the Management members were beginning to rally, and took the floor. The Centrists and Right Moderates were trying the appeal-to-reason approach; that did as much good as trying to put out a Fifth Level forest fire with a hand-extinguisher. Finally, Salgath got a motion of censure against the Management recognized. That means a confidence vote in ten days. Salgath has a rabble of Leftists and dissident Centrists with him; I doubt if he can muster enough votes to overturn the Management, but it's going to make things rough for us."

"Which may be just the reason Salgath started this uproar," Vall suggested.

"That," Tortha Karf said, "is being considered; there is a discreet inquiry being made into Salgath Trod's associates, his sources of income, and so on. Nothing has turned up as yet, but we have hopes."

"I believe," Vall said, "that we have a better chance right on Home Time Line than outtime."

Tortha Karf looked up sharply. "So?" he asked.

Vall was stuffing tobacco into a pipe. "Yes. Chief. We have a big criminal organization — let's call it the Slave Trust, for a convenience-label. The people who run it aren't stupid. The fact that they've been shipping slaves to the Esaron Sector for ten years before we found out about it proves that. So does the speed with which they got rid of this Nebu-hin-Abenoz, right in front of a pair of our detectives. For that matter, so does the speed with which they moved in to exploit this Croutha invasion of Kholghoor Sector India.

"Well, I've studied illegal and subversive organizations all over paratime, and among the really successful ones, there are a few uniform principles. One is cellular organization — small groups, acting in isolation from one another, coöperating with other cells but ignorant of their composition. Another is the principle of no upward contact — leaders contacting their subordinates through contact-blocks and ignorant intermediaries. And another is a willingness to kill off anybody who looks like a potential betrayer or forced witness. The late Nebu-hin-Abenoz, for instance.

"I'll be willing to bet that if we pick up some of these Wizard Traders, say, or a gang that's selling slaves to some Nebu-hin-Abenoz personality on some other time line, and narco-hypnotize them, all they'll be able to do will be name a few immediate associates, and the group leader will know that he's contacted from time to time by some stranger with orders, and that he can make emergency contacts only through some blind accommodation-address. The men who are running this are right on Home Time Line, many of them in positions of prominence, and if we can catch one of them and narco-hyp him, we can start a chain-reaction of disclosures all through this Slave Trust."

"How are we going to get at these top men?" Tortha Karf wanted to know. "Advertise for them on telecast?"

"They'll leave traces; they won't be able to avoid it. I think, right now, that Salgath Trod is one of them. I think there are other prominent politicians, and business people. Look for irregularities and peculiarities in outtime currency-exchange transactions. For instance, to sections in Esaron Sector *obus*. Or big gold bullion transactions."

"Yes. And if they have any really elaborate outtime bases, they'll need equipment that can only be gotten on Home Time Line," Tortha Karf added. "Paratemporal conveyer parts, and field-conductor mesh. You can't just walk into a hardware store and buy that sort of thing."

Dalla leaned forward to drop her cigarette ash into a tray.

"Try looking into the Bureau of Psychological Hygiene," she suggested. "That's where you'll really strike it rich."

Vall and Tortha Karf both turned abruptly and looked at her for an instant.

"Go on," Tortha Karf encouraged. "This sounds interesting."

"The people back of this," Dalla said, "are definitely classifiable as criminals. They may never perform a criminal act themselves, but they give orders for and profit from such acts, and they must possess the motivation and psychology of criminals. We define people as criminals when they suffer from psychological aberrations of an antisocial character, usually paranoid — excessive egoism, disregard for the rights of others, inability to recognize the social necessity for mutual coöperation and confidence. On Home Time Line, we have universal psychological testing, for the purpose of detecting and eliminating such characteristics."

"It seems to have failed in this case," Tortha Karf began, then snapped his fingers. "Of course! How blasted silly can I get, when I'm not trying?"

"Yes, of course," Verkan Vall agreed. "Find out how these people missed being spotted by psychotesting; that'll lead us to *who* missed being tested adequately, and also who got into the Bureau of Psychological Hygiene who didn't belong there."

"I think you ought to give an investigation of the whole Bu-PsychHyg setup very high priority," Dalla said. "A psychotest is only as good as the people who give it, and if we have criminals administering these tests —"

"We have our friends on Executive Council," Tortha Karf said. "I'll see that that point is raised when Council re-convenes." He looked at the clock. "That'll be in three hours, by the way. If it does-n't accomplish another thing, it'll put Salgath Trod in the middle. He can't demand an investigation of the Paratime Police out of one side of his mouth and oppose an investigation of Psychological Hygiene out of the other. Now what else have we to talk about?"

"Those hundred slaves we got off the Esaron Sector," Vall said. "What are we going to do with them? And if we locate the time line the slavers have their bases on, we'll have hundreds, probably thousands, more."

"We can't sort them out and send them back to their own time lines, even if that would be desirable," Tortha Karf decided. "Why, settle them somewhere on the Service Sector. I know, the Paratime Transposition Code limits the Service Sector to natives of time lines below second-order barbarism, but the Paratime Transposition Code has been so badly battered by this business that a few more minor literal infractions here and there won't make any difference. Where are they now?"

"Police Terminal, Nharkan Equivalent."

"Better hold them there, for the time being. We may have to open a new ServSec time line to take care of all the slaves we find, if we can locate the outtime base line these people are using — Vall, this thing's too big to handle as a routine operation, along with our other work. You take charge of it. Set up your headquarters here, and help yourself to anything in the way of personnel and equip-ment you need. And bear in mind that this confidence vote is coming up in ten days — on the morning of One-Seven-Two Day.

I'm not asking for any miracles, but if we don't get this thing cleared up by then, we're in for trouble."

"I realize that, sir. Dalla, you'd better go back to Home Time Line, with the Chief," he said. "There's nothing you can do to help me, here, at present. Get some rest, and then try to wangle an invitation for the two of us to dinner at Thalvan Dras' apartments this evening." He turned back to Tortha Karf. "Even if he never pays any attention to business, Dras still owns Consolidated Outtime Foodstuffs," he said. "He might be able to find out, or help us find out, how the story about those slaves leaked out of his company."

"Well, that won't take much doing," Dalla said. "If there's as much excitement on Home Time Line as I think, Dras would turn somersaults and jump through hoops to get us to one of his dinners, right now."

Salgath Trod pushed the litter of papers and record-tape spools to one side impatiently.

"Well, what else did you expect?" he demanded. "This was the logical next move. BuPsychHyg is supposed to detect anybody who believes in looking out for his own interests first, and condition him into a pious law-abiding sucker. Well, the sacred Bureau of Sucker-Makers slipped up on a lot of us. It's a natural alibi for Tortha Karf."

"It's also a lot of grief for all of us," the young man in the wrap-around tunic added. "I don't want my psychotests reviewed by some duty-struck bigot who can't be reasoned with, and neither do you."

"I'm getting something organized to counter that," Salgath Trod said. "I'm going to attack the whole scientific basis of psycho-testing. There's Dr. Frasthor Klav; he's always contended that what are called criminal tendencies are the result of the individual's total environment, and that psychotesting and personality-analysis are valueless, because the total environment changes from day to day, even from hour to hour —"

"That won't do," the nameless young man who was the messenger of somebody equally nameless retorted. "Frasthor's a crackpot; no reputable psychologist or psychist gives his opinions a moment's consideration. And besides, we don't want to attack Psychological Hygiene. The people in it with whom we can do business are our safeguard; they've given all of us a clean bill of mental health, and we have papers to prove it. What we have to do is to make it appear that that incident on the Esaron Sector is all there is to this, and also involve the Paratime Police themselves. The slavers are all paracops. It isn't the fault of BuPsychHyg, because the Paratime Police have their own psychotesting staff. That's where the trouble is; the paracops haven't been adequately testing their own personnel."

"Now how are you going to do that?" Salgath Trod asked disdainfully.

"You'll take the floor, the first thing tomorrow, and utilize these new revelations about the Wizard Traders. You'll accuse the Paratime Police of being the Wizard Traders themselves. Why not? They have their own paratemporal transposition equipment shops on Police Terminal, they have facilities for manufacturing duplicates of any kind of outtime items, like the firearms, for instance, and they know which time lines on which sectors are being exploited by legitimate paratime traders and which aren't. What's to prevent a gang of unscrupulous paracops from moving in on a few unexploited Kholghoor time lines, buying captives from the Croutha, and shipping them to the Esaron Sector?"

"Then why would they let a thing like this get out?" Salgath Trod inquired.

"Somebody slipped up and moved a lot of slaves onto an exploited Esaron time line. Or, rather, Consolidated Outtime Foodstuffs established a plantation on a time line they were shipping slaves to. Parenthetically, that's what really did happen; the mistake our people made was in not closing out that time line as soon as Consolidated Foodstuffs moved in," the young man said.

"So, this Skordran Kirv, who is a dumb boy who doesn't know what the score is, found these slaves and blatted about it to this Golzan Doth, and Golzan reported it to his company, and it couldn't be hushed up, so now Tortha Karf is trying to scare the public with ghost stories about a gigantic paratemporal conspiracy, to get more appropriations and more power."

"How long do you think I'd get away with that?" Salgath Trod demanded. "I can only stretch parliamentary immunity so far. Sooner or later, I'd have to make formal charges to a special judicial committee, and that would mean narco-hypnosis, and then it would all come out."

"You'll have proof," the young man said. "We'll produce a couple of these Kharandas whom Verkan Vall didn't get hold of. Under narco-hypnosis, they'll testify that they saw a couple of Wizard Traders take their robes off. Under the robes were Paratime Police uniforms. Do you follow me?"

Salgath Trod made a noise of angry disgust.

"That's ridiculous! I suppose these Kharandas will be given what is deludedly known as memory obliteration, and a set of pseudo-memories; how long do you think that would last? About three ten-days. There is no such thing as memory obliteration; there's memory-suppression, and pseudo-memory overlay. You can't get behind that with any quickie narco-hypnosis in the back room of any police post, I'll admit that," he said. "But a skilled psychist can discover, inside of five minutes, when a narco-hypno-tized subject is carrying a load of false memories, and in time, and not too much time, all that top layer of false memories and block-ages can be peeled off. And then where would we be?"

"Now wait a minute, Councilman. This isn't just something I dreamed up," the visitor said. "This was decided upon at the top. At the very top."

"I don't care whose idea it was," Salgath Trod snapped. "The whole thing is idiotic, and I won't have anything to do with it."

The visitor's face froze. All the respect vanished from his man-ner and tone; his voice was like ice cakes grating together in a winter river.

"Look, Salgath; this is an Organization order," he said. "You don't refuse to obey Organization orders, and you don't quit the Organization. Now get smart, big boy; do what you're told to." He took a spool of record tape from his pocket and laid it on the desk. "Outline for your speech; put it in your own words, but follow it exactly." He stood watching Salgath Trod for a moment. "I won't bother telling you what'll happen to you if you don't," he added. "You can figure that out for yourself."

With that, he turned and went out the private door. For a while, Salgath Trod sat staring after him. Once he put his hand out toward the spool, then jerked it back as though the thing were radioactive. Once he looked at the clock; it was just 1600.

The green aircar settled onto the landing stage; Verkan Vall, on the front seat beside the driver, opened the door.

"Want me to call for you later, Assistant Verkan?" the driver asked.

"No thank you, Drenth. My wife and I are going to a dinner-party, and we'll probably go night-clubbing afterward. Tomorrow morning, all the anti-Management commentators will be yakking about my carousing around when I ought to be battling the Slave Trust. No use advertising myself with an official car, and giving them a chance to add, 'at public expense.'"

"Well, have some fun while you can," the driver advised, reaching for the car-radio phone. "Want me to check you in here, sir?"

"Yes, if you will. Thank you. Drenth."

Kandagro, his human servant, admitted him to the apartment six floors down.

"Mistress Dalla is dressing," he said. "She asked me to tell you that you are invited to dinner, this evening, with Thalvan Dras at his apartment."

Vall nodded. "Ill talk to her about it now," he said. "Lay out my dress uniform: short jacket, boots and breeches, and needler."

"Yes, master: I'll go lay out your things and get your bath ready."

The servant turned and went into the alcove which gave access to the dressing rooms, turning right into Vall's. Vall followed him, turning left into his wife's.

"Oh, Dalla!" he called.

"In here!" her voice came out of her bathroom.

He passed through the dressing room, to find her stretched on a plastic-sheeted couch, while her maid, Rendarra, was rubbing her body vigorously with some pungent-smelling stuff about the consistency of machine-grease. Her face was masked in the stuff, and her hair was covered with an elastic cap. He had always suspected that beauty was the real feminine religion, from the willingness of its devotees to submit to martyrdom for it. She wiggled a hand at him in greeting.

"How did it go?" she asked.

"So-so. I organized myself a sort of miniature police force within a police force and I have liaison officers in every organization down to Sector Regional so that I can be informed promptly in case anything new turns up anywhere. What's been happening on Home Time Line? I picked up a news-summary at Paratime Police Headquarters; it seems that a lot more stuff has leaked out. Kholghoor

Sector, Wizard Traders and all. How'd it happen?"

Dalla rolled over to allow Rendarra to rub the blue-green grease on her back.

"Consolidated Outtime Foodstuffs let a gang of reporters in, today. I think they're afraid somebody will accuse them of complicity, and they want to get their side of it before the public. All our crowd are off that Time line except a couple of detectives at the plantation."

"I know." He smiled; Dalla was thinking of the Paratime Police as "our crowd" now. "How about this dinner at Dras' place?"

"Oh, that was easy." She shifted position again. "I just called Dras up and told him that our vacation was off, and he invited us before I could begin hinting. What are you going to wear?"

"Short-jacket greens; I can carry a needler with that uniform, even wear it at the table. I don't think it's smart for me to run around unarmed, even on Home Time Line. Especially on Home Time Line," he amended. "When's this affair going to start, and how long will Rendarra take to get that goo off you?"

Salgath Trod left his aircar at the top landing stage of his apartment building and sent it away to the hangars under robot control; he glanced about him as he went toward the antigrav shaft. There were a dozen vehicles in the air above; any of them might have followed him from the Paratime Building. He had no doubt that he had been under constant surveillance from the moment the nameless messenger had delivered the Organization's ultimatum. Until he delivered that speech, the next morning, or manifested an intention of refusing to do so, however, he would be safe. After that —

Alone in his office, he had reviewed the situation point by point, and then gone back and reviewed it again; the conclusion was inescapable. The Organization had ordered him to make an accusation which he himself knew to be false; that was the first premise. The conclusion was that he would be killed as soon as he had made it. That was the trouble with being mixed up with that kind of people — you were expendable, and sooner or later, they would decide that they would have to expend you. And what could you do?

To begin with, an accusation of criminal malfeasance made

against a Management or Paratime Commission agency on the floor of Executive Council was tantamount to an accusation made in court; automatically, the accuser became a criminal prosecutor, and would have to repeat his accusation under narco-hypnosis. Then the whole story would come out, bit by bit, back to its beginning in that first illegal deal in Indo-Turanian opium, diverted from trade with the Khiftan Sector and sold on Second Level Luvarian Empire Sector, and the deals in radioactive poisons, and the slave trade. He would be able to name few names — the Organization kept its activities too well compartmented for that — but he could talk of things that had happened, and when, and where, and on what paratemporal areas.

No. The Organization wouldn't let that happen, and the only way it could be prevented would be by the death of Salgath Trod, as soon as he had made his speech. All the talk of providing him with corroborative evidence was silly; it had been intended to lead him more trustingly to the slaughter. They'd kill him, of course, in some way that would be calculated to substantiate the story he would no longer be able to repudiate. The killer, who would be promptly rayed dead by somebody else, would wear a Paratime Police uniform, or something like that. That was of no importance, however; by then, he'd be beyond caring.

One of his three ServSec Prole servants — the slim brown girl who was his housekeeper and hostess, and also his mistress — admitted him to the apartment. He kissed her perfunctorily and closed the door behind him.

"You're tired," she said. "Let me call Nindrandigro and have him bring you chilled wine; lie down and rest until dinner."

"No, no; I want brandy." He went to a cellaret and got out a decanter and goblet, pouring himself a drink. "How soon will dinner be ready?"

The brown girl squeezed a little golden globe that hung on a chain around her neck; a tiny voice, inside it, repeated: "Eighteen twenty-three ten, eighteen twenty-three eleven, eighteen twenty-three twelve —"

"In half an hour. It's still in the robo-chef," she told him.

He downed half the goblet-full, set it down, and went to a painting, a brutal scarlet and apple-green abstraction, that hung on the wall. Swinging it aside and revealing the safe behind it, he used his identity-sigil, took out a wad of Paratemporal Exchange Bank notes and gave them to the girl.

"Here, Zinganna; take these, and take Nindrandigro and Calilla out for the evening. Go where you can all have a good time, and don't come back till after midnight. There will be some business transacted here, and I want them out of this. Get them out of here as soon as you can; I'll see to the dinner myself. Spend all of that you want to."

The girl riffled through the wad of banknotes. "Why, *thank* you, Trod!" She threw her arms around his neck and kissed him enthusiastically. "I'll go tell them at once."

"And have a good time, Zinganna; have the best time you possibly can," he told her, embracing and kissing her. "Now, get out of here; I have to keep my mind on business."

When she had gone, he finished his drink and poured another. He drew and checked his needler. Then, after checking the window-shielding and activating the outside viewscreens, he lit a cheroot and sat down at the desk, his goblet and his needler in front of him, to wait until the servants were gone.

There was only one way out alive. He knew that, and yet he needed brandy, and a great deal of mental effort, to steel himself for it. Psycho-rehabilitation was a dreadful thing to face. There would be almost a year of unremitting agony, physical and mental, worse than a Khiftan torture rack. There would be the shame of having his innermost secrets poured out of him by the psychotherapists, and, at the end, there would emerge someone who would not be Salgath Trod, or anybody like Salgath Trod, and he would have to learn to know this stranger, and build a new life for him.

In one of the viewscreens, he saw the door to the service hallway open. Zinganna, in a black evening gown and a black velvet cloak, and Calilla, the housemaid, in what she believed to be a reasonable facsimile of fashionable First Level dress, and Nindrandigro, in one of his master's evening suits, emerged. Salgath Trod waited until they had gone down the hall to the antigrav shaft, and then he turned on the visiphone, checked the security, set it for sealed beam communication, and punched out a combination.

A girl in a green tunic looked out of the screen.

"Paratime Police," she said. "Office of Chief Tortha."

"I am Executive Councilman Salgath Trod," he told her. "I am, and for the past fifteen years have been, criminally involved with the organization responsible for the slave trade which recently came to light on Third Level Esaron. I give myself up unconditionally; I am willing to make full confession under narco-hypnosis, and will accept whatever disposition of my case is lawfully judged fit. You'll have to send an escort for me; I might start from my apartment alone, but I'd be killed before I got to your headquarters —"

The girl, who had begun to listen in the bored manner of public servants phone girls, was staring wide-eyed.

"Just a moment, Councilman Salgath; I'll put you through to Chief Tortha."

The dinner lacked a half hour of being served; Thalvan Dras' guests loitered about the drawing room, sampling appetizers and chilled drinks and chatting in groups. It wasn't the artistic crowd usual at Thalvan Dras' dinners; most of the guests seemed to be business or political people. Thalvan Dras had gotten Vall and Dalla into the small group around him, along with pudgy, infantile-faced Brogoth Zaln, his confidential secretary, and Javrath Brend, his financial attorney.

"I don't see why they're making such a fuss about it," one of the Banking Cartel people was saying. "Causing a lot of public excitement all out of proportion to the importance of the affair. After all, those people were slaves on their own time line, and if anything, they're much better off on the Esaron Sector than they would be as captives of the Croutha. As far as that goes, what's the difference between that and the way we drag these Fourth Level Primitive Sector-Complex people off to Fifth Level Service Sector to work for us?"

"Oh, there's a big difference, Farn," Javrath Brend said. "We recruit those Fourth Level Primitives out of probability worlds of Stone Age savagery, and transpose them to our own Fifth Level time lines, practically outtime extensions of the Home Time Line. There's absolutely no question of the Paratime Secret being compromised."

"Beside, we need a certain amount of human labor, for tasks requiring original thought and decision that are beyond the ability of robots, and most of it is work our Citizens simply wouldn't perform," Thalvan Dras added.

"Well, from a moral standpoint, wouldn't these Esaron Sector people who buy the slaves justify slavery in the same terms?" a woman whom Vall had identified as a Left Moderate Council Member asked.

"There's still a big difference," Dalla told her. "The ServSec Proles aren't beaten or tortured or chained; we don't break up families or separate friends. When we recruit Fourth Level Primitives, we take whole tribes, and they come willingly. And —"

One of Thalvan Dras' black-liveried human servants, of the class under discussion, approached Vall.

"A visiphone call for your lordship," he whispered. "Chief Tortha Karf calling. If your lordship will come this way —"

In a screen-booth outside, Vall found Tortha Karf looking out of the screen; he was seated at his desk, fiddling with a gold multicolor pen.

"Oh, Vall; something interesting has just come up." He spoke in a voice of forced calmness. "I can't go into it now, but you'll want to hear about it. I'm sending a car for you. Better bring Dalla along; she'll want in on it, too."

"Right; we'll be on the top south-west landing stage in a few minutes."

Dalla was still heatedly repudiating any resemblance between the normal First Level methods of labor-recruitment and the activities of the Wizard Traders; she had just finished the story of the woman whose child had been brained when Vall rejoined the group.

"Dras, I'm awfully sorry," he said. "This is the second time in succession that Dalla and I have had to bolt away from here, but policemen are like doctors — always on call, and consequently unreliable guests. While you're feasting, think commiseratingly of Dalla and me; we'll probably be having a sandwich and a cup of coffee somewhere."

"I'm terribly sorry." Thalvan Dras replied. "We had all been looking forward — Well! Brogoth, have a car called for Vall and Dalla."

"Police car coming for us; it's probably on the landing stage now," Vall said. "Well, good-by, everybody. Coming, Dalla?"

*   *   *

They had a few minutes to wait, under the marquee, before the green police aircar landed and came rolling across the rain-wet surface of the landing stage. Crossing to it and opening the rear door, he put Dalla in and climbed in after her, slamming the door. It was only then that he saw Tortha Karf hunched down in the rear seat. He motioned them to silence, and did not speak until the car was rising above the building.

"I wanted to fill you in on this, as soon as possible," he said. "Your hunch about Salgath Trod was good; just a few minutes before I called you, he called me. He says this slave trade is the work of something he calls the Organization; says he's been taking orders from them for years. His attack on the Management and motion for a censure-vote were dictated from Organization top echelon. Now he's convinced that they're going to force him to make false accusations against the Paratime Police and then kill him before he's compelled to repeat his charges under narco-hypnosis. So he's offered to surrender and trade information for protection."

"How much does he know?" Vall asked.

Tortha Karf shook his head. "Not as much as he claims to, I suppose; he wouldn't want to reduce his own trade-in value. But he's been involved in this thing for the last fifteen years, and with his political prominence, he'd know quite a lot."

"We can protect him from his own gang; can we protect him from psycho-rehabilitation?"

"No, and he knows it. He's willing to accept that. He seems to think that death at the hands of his own associates is the only other alternative. Probably right, too."

The floodlighted green towers of the Paratime Building were wheeling under them as they circled down.

"Why would they sacrifice a valuable accomplice like Salgath Trod, in order to make a transparently false accusation against us?" Vall wondered.

"Ha, that's our new rookie cop's idea!" Tortha Karf chuckled, nodding toward Dalla. "We got Zortan Harn to introduce an urgent-business motion to appoint a committee to investigate BuPsych-Hyg, this morning. The motion passed, and this is the reaction to it. The Organization's scared. Just as Dalla predicted, they don't want us finding out how people with potentially criminal characteristics missed being spotted by psychotesting. Salgath Trod is being sacrificed to block or delay that."

Vall nodded as the wheels bumped on the landing stage and the antigrav field went off. That was the sort of thing that happened when you started on a really fruitful line of investigation. They got out and hurried over under the marquee, the car lifting and moving off toward the hangars. This was the real break; no matter how this Organization might be compartmented, a man like Salgath Trod would know a great deal. He would name names, and the bearers of those names, arrested and narco-hypnotized, would name other names, in a perfect chain reaction of confessions and betrayals.

Another police car had landed just ahead of them, and three men were climbing out; two were in Paratime Police green, and the third, hand-cuffed, was in Service Sector Proletarian garb. At first, Vall though that Salgath Trod had been brought in disguised as a Prole prisoner, and then he saw that the prisoner was short and stocky, not at all like the slender and elegant politician. The two officers who had brought him in were talking to a lieutenant, Sothran Barth, outside the antigrav shaft kiosk. As Vall and Tortha Karf and Dalla walked over, the car which had brought them lifted out.

"Something that just came in from Industrial Twenty-four, Chief," Lieutenant Sothran said in answer to Tortha Karf's question. "May be for Assistant Verkan's desk."

"He's a Prole named Yandragno, sir," one of the policemen said. "Industrial Sector Constabulary grabbed him peddling Martian hellweed cigarettes to the girls in a textile mill at Kangabar Equivalent. Captain Jamzar thinks he may have gotten them from somebody in the Organization."

A little warning bell began ringing in the back of Verkan Vall's mind, but at first he could not consciously identify the cause of his suspicions. He looked the two policemen and their prisoner over carefully, but could see nothing visibly wrong with them. Then another car came in for a landing and rolled over under the marquee; the door opened, and a police officer got out, followed by an elegantly dressed civilian whom he recognized at once as Salgath Trod. A second policeman was emerging from the car when Vall suddenly realized what it was that had disturbed him.

It had been Salgath Trod, himself, less than half an hour ago, who had introduced the term, "the Organization," to the Paratime Police. At that time, if these people were what they claimed to be, they would have been in transposition from Industrial Twenty-four, on the Fifth Level. Immediately, he reached for his needler. He was clearing it of the holster when things began happening.

The handcuffs fell from the "prisoner's" wrists; he jerked a neutron-disruption blaster from under his jacket. Vall, his needler already drawn, rayed the fellow dead before he could aim it, then saw that the two pseudo-policemen had drawn their needlers and were aiming in the direction of Salgath Trod. There were no flashes or reports; only the spot of light that had winked on and off under Vall's rear sight had told him that his weapon had been activated. He saw it appear again as the sights centered on one of the "policemen." Then he saw the other imposter's needler aimed at himself. That was the last thing he expected ever to see, in that life; he tried to shift his own weapon, and time seemed frozen, with his arm barely moving. Then there was a white blur as Dalla's cloak moved in front of him, and the needler dropped from the fingers of the disguised murderer. Time went back to normal for him; he safetied his own weapon and dropped it, jumping forward.

He grabbed the fellow in the green uniform by the nose with his left hand, and punched him hard in the pit of the stomach with his right fist. The man's mouth flew open, and a green capsule, the size and shape of a small bean, flew out. Pushing Dalla aside before she would step on it, he kicked the murderer in the stomach, doubling him over, and chopped him on the base of the skull with the edge of his hand. The pseudo-policeman dropped senseless.

With a handful of handkerchief-tissue from his pocket, he picked up the disgorged capsule, wrapping it carefully after making sure that it was unbroken. Then he looked around. The other two assassins were dead. Tortha Karf, who had been looking at the man in Proletarian dress whom Vall had killed first, turned, looked in another direction, and then cursed. Vall followed his eyes, and cursed also. One of the two policemen who had gotten out of the aircar was dead, too, and so was the all-important witness, Salgath Trod — as dead as Nebu-hin-Abenoz, a hundred thousand para-years away.

The whole thing had ended within thirty seconds; for about half as long, everybody waited, poised in a sort of action-vacuum, for something else to happen. Dalla had dropped the shoulder-bag with which she had clubbed the prisoner's needler out of his hand, and caught up the fallen weapon. When she saw that the man was down and motionless, she laid it aside and began picking up the glittering or silken trifles that had spilled from the burst bag. Vall retrieved his own weapon, glanced over it, and holstered it. Sothran Barth, the lieutenant in charge of the landing stage, was bawling orders, and men were coming out of the ready-room and piling into vehicles to pursue the aircar which had brought the assassins.

"Barth!" Vall called. "Have you a hypodermic and a sleep-drug ampoule? Well, give this boy a shot; he's only impact-stunned. Be careful of him; he's important." He glanced around the landing-stage. "Fact is, he's all we have to show for this business."

Then he stooped to help Dalla gather her things, picking up a few of them — a lighter, a tiny crystal perfume flask, miraculously unbroken, a face-powder box which had sprung open and spilled half its contents. He handed them to her, while Sothran Barth bent over the prisoner and gave him an injection, then went to the body of the other pseudo-policeman, forcing open his mouth. In his cheek, still unbroken, was a second capsule, which he added to the first. Tortha Karf was watching him.

"Same gang that killed that Carera slaver on Esaron Sector?" he asked. "Of course, exactly the same general procedure. Let's have a look at the other one."

The man in Proletarian dress must have had his capsule between his molars when he had been killed; it was broken, and there was a brownish discoloration and chemical odor in his mouth.

"Second time we've had a witness killed off under our noses," Tortha Karf said. "We're going to have to smarten up in a hurry."

"Here's one of us who doesn't have to, much," Vall said, nodding toward Dalla. "She knocked a needler out of one man's hand, and we took him alive. The Force owes her a new shoulder-bag: she spoiled that one using it for a club."

"Best shoulder-bag we can find you, Dalla," Tortha Karf promised. "You're promoted, herewith, to Special Chief's Assistant's Special Assistant — You know, this Organization murder-section is good; they could kill anybody. It won't be long before they assign a squad to us. Blast it, I don't want to have to go around body-guarded like a Fourth Level dictator, but —"

A detective came out of the control room and approached.

"Screen call for you, sir," he told Tortha Karf. "One of the news services wants a comment on a story they've just picked up that we've illegally arrested Councilman Salgath and are holding him incommunicado and searching his apartment."

"That's the Organization," Vall said. "They don't know how their boys made out; they're hoping we'll tell them."

"No comment," Tortha Karf said. "Call the girl on my switchboard and tell her to answer any other news-service calls. We have nothing to say at this time, but there will be a public statement at . . . at 2330," he decided after a glance at his watch. "That'll give us time to agree on a publicity line to adopt. Lieutenant Sothran! Take charge up here. Get all these bodies out of sight somewhere, including those of Councilman Salgath and Detective Malthor. Don't let anybody talk about this; put a blackout on the whole story. Vall, you and Dalla and . . . oh, you, over there; take the prisoner down to my office. Sothran, any reports from any of the cars that were chasing that fake police car?"

Verkan Vall and Dalla were sitting behind Tortha Karf's desk; Vall was issuing orders over the intercom and talking to the detectives who had remained at Salgath Trod's apartment by visiscreen; Dalla was sorting over the things she had spilled when her bag had burst. They both looked up as Tortha Karf came in and joined them.

"The prisoner's still under the drug," the Chief said. "He'll be out for a couple of hours; the psych-techs want to let him come out of it naturally and sleep naturally for a while before they give him a hypno. He's not a ServSec Prole; uncircumcised, never had any syntho-enzyme shots or immunizations, and none of the longevity operations or grafts. Same thing for the two stiffs. And no identity records on any of the three."

"The men at Salgath's apartment say that his housekeeper and his two servants checked out through the house conveyer for ServSec One-Six-Five, at about 1830," Vall said. "There's a Prole entertainment center on that time line. I suppose Salgath gave them the evening off before he called you."

Tortha Karf nodded. "I suppose you ordered them picked up. The news services are going wild about this. I had to make a preliminary statement, to the effect that Salgath Trod was not arrested, came to Headquarters of his own volition, and is under no restraint whatever."

"Except, of course, a slight case of rigor mortis," Dalla added. "Did you mention that, Chief?"

"No, I didn't." Tortha Karf looked as though he had quinine in his mouth. "Vall, how in blazes are we going to handle this?"

"We ought to keep Salgath's death hushed up, as long as we can," Vall said. "The Organization doesn't know positively what happened here; that's why they're handing out tips to the news services. Let's try to make them believe he's still alive and talking."

"How can we do it?"

"There ought to be somebody on the Force close enough to Salgath Trod's anthropometric specifications that our cosmeticians could work him over into a passable impersonation. Our story is that Salgath is on PolTerm, undergoing narco-hypnosis. We will produce an audio-visual of him as soon as he is out of narco-hyp. That will give us time to fix up an impersonator; We'll need a lot of sound-recordings of Salgath Trod's voice, of course —"

"I'll take care of the Home Time Line end of it; as soon as we get you an impersonator, you go to work with him. Now, let's see whom we can depend on to help us with this. Lovranth Rolk, of course; Home Time Line section of the Paratime Code Enforcement Division. And —"

Verkan Vall and Dalla and Tortha Karf and four or five others looked across the desk and to the end of the room as the telecast screen broke into a shifting light-pattern and then cleared. The face of the announcer appeared; a young woman.

"And now, we bring you the statement which Chief Tortha of the Paratime Police has promised for this time. This portion of the program was audio-visually recorded at Paratime Police Headquarters earlier this evening."

Tortha Karf's face appeared on the screen. His voice began an announcement of how Executive Councilman Salgath Trod had called him by visiphone, admitting to complicity in the recently-discovered paratemporal slave-trade.

"Here is a recording of Councilman Salgath's call to me from his apartment to my office at 1945 this evening."

The screen-image shattered into light-shards and rebuilt itself: Salgath Trod, at his desk in the library of his apartment, the brandy-goblet and the needler within reach, appeared. He began to speak: from time to time the voice of Tortha Karf interrupted, questioning or prompting him.

"You understand that this confession renders you liable to psycho-rehabilitation?" Tortha Karf asked.

Yes, Councilman Salgath understood that.

"And you agree to come voluntarily to Paratime Police Headquarters, and you will voluntarily undergo narco-hypnotic interrogation?"

Yes, Salgath Trod agreed to that.

"I am now terminating the playback of Councilman Salgath's call to me," Tortha Karf said, re-appearing on the screen. "At this point Councilman Salgath began making a statement about his criminal activities, which we have on record. Because he named a number of his criminal associates, whom we have no intention of warning, this portion of Councilman Salgath's call cannot at this time be made public. We have no intention of having any of these suspects escape, or of giving their associates an opportunity to murder them to prevent their furnishing us with additional information. Incidentally, there was an attempt, made on the landing stage of Paratime Police Headquarters, to murder Councilman Salgath, when he was brought here guarded by Paratime Police officers —"

He went on to give a colorful and, as far as possible, truthful, account of the attack by the two pseudo-policemen and their pseudo-prisoner. As he told it, however, all three had been killed before they could accomplish their purpose, one of them by Salgath Trod himself.

The image of Tortha Karf was replaced by a view of the three assassins lying on the landing stage. They all looked dead, even the one who wasn't; there was nothing to indicate that he was merely drugged. Then, one after another, their faces were shown in closeup, while Tortha Karf asked for close attention and memorization.

"We believe that these men were Fifth Level Proles; we think that they were under hypnotic influence or obeying posthypnotic commands when they made their suicidal attack. If any of you have ever seen any of these men before, it is your duty to inform the Paratime Police."

*   *   *

That ended it. Tortha Karf pressed a button in front of him and the screen went dark. The spectators relaxed.

"Well! Nothing like being sincere with the public, is there?" Della commented. "I'll remember this the next time I tune in a Management public statement."

"In about five minutes," one of the bureau-chiefs, said, "all hell is going to break loose. I think the whole thing is crazy!"

"I hope you have somebody who can give a convincing impersonation," Lovranth Rolk said.

"Yes. A field agent named Kostran Galth," Tortha Karf said. "We ran the personal description cards for the whole Force through the machine; Kostran checked to within one-twentieth of one per cent; he's on Police Terminal, now, coming by rocket from Ravvanan Equivalent. We ought to have the whole thing ready for telecast by 1730 tomorrow."

"He can't learn to imitate Salgath's voice convincingly in that time, with all the work the cosmeticians'll have to be doing on him," Dalla said.

"Make up a tape of Salgath's own voice, out of that pile of recordings we got at his apartment, and what we can get out of the news file." Vall said. "We have phoneticists who can split syllables and splice them together. Kostran will deliver his speech in dumbshow, and we'll dub the sound in and telecast them as one. I've messaged PolTerm to get to work on that; they can start as soon as we have the speech written."

"The more it succeeds now, the worse the blow-up will be when we finally have to admit that Salgath was killed here tonight," the Chief Inter-officer Coördinator, Zostha Olv said. "We'd better have something to show the public to justify that."

"Yes, we had," Tortha Karf agreed. "Vall, how about the Kholghoor Sector operation. How far's Ranthar Jard gotten toward locating one of those Wizard Trader time lines?"

"Not very far," Vall admitted. "He has it pinned down to the sub-sector, but the belt seems to be one we haven't any information at all for. Never been any legitimate penetration by paratimers. He has his own hagiologists, and a couple borrowed from Outtime Religious Institute; they've gotten everything the slaves can give them on that. About the only thing to do is start random observation with boomerang-balls."

"Over about a hundred thousand time lines," Zostha Olv

scoffed. He was an old man, even for his long-lived race; he had a thin nose and a narrow, bitter, mouth. "And what will he look for?"

"Croutha with guns." Tortha Karf told him, then turned to Vall. "Can't he narrow it more than that? What have his experts been getting out of those slaves?"

"That I don't know, to date." Vall looked at the clock. "I'll find out, though; I'll transpose to Police Terminal and call him up. And Skordran Kirv. No. Vulthor Tharn; it'd hurt the old fellow's feelings if I by-passed him and went to one of his subordinates. Half an hour each way, and at most another hour talking to Ranthar and Vulthor; there won't be anything doing here for two hours." He rose. "See you when I get back."

Dalla had turned on the telescreen again; after tuning out a dance orchestra and a comedy show, she got the image of an angry-faced man in evening clothes.

". . . And I'm going to demand a full investigation, as soon as Council convenes tomorrow morning!" he was shouting. "This whole story is a preposterous insult to the integrity of the entire Executive Council, your elected representatives, and it shows the criminal lengths to which this would-be dictator, Tortha Karf, and his jackal Verkan Vall will go —"

"So long, jackal." Dalla called to him as he went out.

He spent the half-hour transposition to Police Terminal sleeping. Paratime-transpositions and rocket-flights seemed to be his only chance to get any sleep. He was still sleepy when he sat down in front of the radio telescreen behind his duplicate of Tortha Karf's desk and put through a call to Nharkan Equivalent. It was 0600 in India; the Sector Regional Deputy Subchief who was holding down Ranthar Jard's desk looked equally sleepy; he had a mug of coffee in front of him, and a brown-paper cigarette in his mouth.

"Oh, hello, Assistant Verkan. Want me to call Subchief Ranthar?"

"Is he sleeping? Then for mercy's sake don't. What's the present status of the investigation?"

"Well, we were dropping boomerang balls yesterday, while we had sun to mask the return-flashes. Nothing. The Croutha have taken the city of Sohram, just below the big bend of the river. Tomorrow, when we have sunlight, we're going to start boomerang-balling the central square. We may get something."

"The Wizard Traders'll be moving in near there, about now," Vall said. "The Croutha ought to have plenty of merchandise for them. Have you gotten anything more done on narrowing down the possible area?"

The deputy bit back a yawn and reached for his coffee mug.

"The experts have just about pumped these slaves empty," he said. "The local religion is a mess. Seems to have started out as a Great Mother cult; then it picked up a lot of gods borrowed from other peoples; then it turned into a dualistic monotheism; then it picked up a lot of minor gods and devils — new devils usually gods of the older pantheon. And we got a lot of gossip about the feudal wars and faction-fights among the nobility, and so on, all garbled, because these people are peasants who only knew what went on on the estate of their own lord."

"What did go on there?" Vall asked. "Ask them about recent improvements, new buildings, new fields cleared, new paddies flooded, that sort of thing. And pick out a few of the highest IQ's from both time lines, and have them locate this estate on a large-scale map, and draw plans showing the location of buildings, fields and other visible features. If you have to, teach them mapping and sketching by hypno-mech. And then drop about five hundred to a thousand boomerang balls, at regular intervals, over the whole paratemporal area. When you locate a time line that gives you a picture to correspond to their description, boomerang the main square in Sohram over the whole belt around it, to find Croutha with firearms."

The deputy looked at him for a moment then gulped more coffee.

"Can do, Assistant Verkan. I think I'll send somebody to wake up Subchief Ranthar, right now. Want to talk to him."

"Won't be necessary. You're recording this call, of course? Then play it back to him. And get cracking with the slaves; you want enough information out of them to enable you to start boomerang balling as soon as the sun's high enough."

He broke off the connection and sent out for coffee for himself. Then he put through a call to Novilan Equivalent, in western North America.

It was 1530, there, when he got Vulthor Tharn on the screen.

"Good afternoon. Assistant Verkan. I suppose you're calling about the slave business. I've turned the entire matter over to Field Agent Skordran; gave him a temporary rank of Deputy Subchief. That's subject to your approval and Chief Tortha's, of course —"

"Make the appointment permanent," Vall said. "I'll have a confirmation along from Chief Tortha directly. And let me talk to him now, if you please. Subchief Vulthor."

"Yes, sir. Switching you over now." The screen went into a beautiful burst of abstract art, and cleared, after a while, with Skordran Kirv looking out of it.

"Hello, Deputy Skordran, and congratulations. What's come up since we had Nebu-hin-Abenoz cut out from under us?"

"We went in on that time line, that same night, with an airboat and made a recon in the hills back of Careba. Scared the fear of Safar into a party of Caleras while we were working at low altitude, by the way. We found the conveyer-head site: hundred-foot circle with all the grass and loose dirt transposed off it and a pole pen, very unsanitary where about two-three hundred slaves would be kept at a time. No indications of use in the last ten days. We did some pretty thorough boomeranging on that spatial equivalent over a couple of thousand time lines and found thirty more of them. I believe the slavers have closed out the whole Esaron Sector operation, at least temporarily."

That was what he'd been afraid of; he hoped they wouldn't do the same thing on the Kholghoor Sector.

"Let me have the designations of the time lines on which you found conveyer heads," he said.

"Just a moment, Chief's Assistant; I'll photoprint them to you. Set for reception?"

Vall opened a slide under the screen and saw that the photoprint film was in place, then closed it again, nodding. Skordran Kirv fed a sheet of paper into his screen cabinet and his arm moved forward out of the picture.

"On, sir," he said. He and Vall counted ten seconds together, and then Skordran Kirv said: "Through to you." Vall pressed a lever under his screen, and a rectangle of microcopy print popped out.

"That's about all I have, sir. Want me to keep my troops ready here, or shall I send them somewhere else?"

"Keep them ready, Kirv," Vall told him. "You may need them before long. Call you later."

He put the microcopy in an enlarger, and carried the enlarged print with him to the conveyer room. There was something odd about the list of time line designations. They were expressed numerically, in First Level notation; extremely short groups of symbols capable of exact expression of almost inconceivably enormous numbers. Vall had only a general-education smattering of mathematics — enough to qualify him for the chair of Higher Mathematics at any university on, say, the Fourth Level Europo-American Sector — and he could not identify the peculiarity, but he could recognize that there existed some sort of pattern. Shoving in the starting lever, he relaxed in one of the chairs, waiting for the transposition field to build up around him, and fell asleep before the mesh dome of the conveyer had vanished. He woke, the list of time line designations in his hand, when the conveyor rematerialized on Home Time Line. Putting it in his pocket, he hurried to an antigrav shaft and floated up to the floor on which Tortha Karf's office was.

Tortha Karf was asleep in his chair; Dalla was eating a dinner that had been brought in to her — something better than the sandwich and mug of coffee Vall had mentioned to Thalvan Dras. Several of the bureau chiefs who had been there when he had gone out had left, and the psychist who had taken charge of the prisoner was there.

"I think he's coming out of the drug, now," he reported. "Still asleep, though. We want him to waken naturally before we start on him. They'll call me as soon as he shows signs of stirring."

"The Opposition's claiming, now, that we drugged and hypnotized Salgath into making that visiscreen confession," Dalla said. "Can you think of any way you could do that without making the subject incapable of lying?"

"Pseudo-memories," the psychist said. "It would take about three times as long as the time between Salgath Trod's departure from his apartment and the time of the telecast, though —"

"You know much higher math?" Vall asked the psychist.

"Well, enough to handle my job. Neuron-synapse inter-relations, memory-and-association patterns, that kind of thing, all have to be expressed mathematically."

Vall nodded and handed him the time-line designation list.

"See any kind of a pattern there?" he asked.

The psychist looked at the paper and blanked his face as he drew on hypnotically-acquired information.

"Yes. I'd say that all the numbers are related in some kind of a series to some other number. Simplified down to kindergarten level, say the difference between A and B is, maybe, one-decillionth of the difference between X and A, and the difference between B and C is one-decillionth of the difference between X and B, and so on —"

A voice came out of one of the communication boxes:

"Dr. Nentrov; the patient's out of the drug, and he's beginning to stir about."

"That's it," the psychist said. "I have to run." He handed the sheet back to Vall, took a last drink from his coffee cup, and bolted out of the room.

Dalla picked up the sheet of paper and looked at it. Vall told her what it was.

"If those time lines are in regular series, they relate to the base line of operations," she said. "Maybe you can have that worked out. I can see how it would be; a stated interval between the Esaron Sector lines, to simplify transposition control settings."

"That was what I was thinking. It's not quite as simple as Dr. Nentrov expressed it, but that could be the general idea. We might be able to work out the location of the base line from that. There seems to be a break in the number sequence in here; that would be the time line Skordran Kirv found those slaves on." He reached for the pipe he had left on the desk when he had gone to Police Terminal and began filling it.

A little later, a buzzer sounded and a light came on on one of the communication boxes. He flipped the switch and said, "Verkan Vall here." Sothran Barth's voice came cut of the box.

"They've just brought in Salgath Trod's servants. Picked them up as they came out of the house conveyer at the apartment building. I don't believe they know what's happened."

Vall flipped a switch and twiddled a dial; a viewscreen lit up, showing the landing stage. The police car had just landed: one detective had gotten out, and was helping the girl, Zinganna, who had been Salgath Trod's housekeeper and mistress, to descend. She was really beautiful. Vall thought: rather tall, slender, with dark eyes and a creamy light-brown skin. She wore a black cloak, and, under it, a black and silver evening gown. A single jewel twinkled in her black hair. She could have very easily passed for a woman of his own race.

The housemaid and the butler were a couple of entirely different articles. Both were about four or five generations from Fourth Level Primitive savagery. The maid, in garishly cheap finery, was big-boned and heavy-bodied, with red-brown hair; she looked like a member of one of the northern European reindeer-herding peoples who had barely managed to progress as far as the bow and arrow. The butler was probably a mixture of half a dozen primitive races; he was wearing one of his late master's evening suits, a bright mellow-pink, which was distinctly unflattering to his complexion.

The sound-pickup was too far away to give him what they were saying, but the butler and maid were waving their arms and protesting vehemently. One of the detectives took the woman by the arm; she jerked it loose and aimed a backhand slap at him. He blocked it on his forearm. Immediately, the girl in black turned and said something to her, and she subsided. Vall said, into the box:

"Barth, have the girl in the black cloak brought down to Number Four Interview Room. Put the other two in separate detention cubicles; we'll talk to them later." He broke the connection and got to his feet. "Come on, Dalla. I want you to help me with the girl."

"Just try and stop me," Dalla told him. "Any interviews you have with that little item, I want to sit in on."

The Proletarian girl, still guarded by a detective, had already been placed in the interview room. The detective nodded to Vall, tried to suppress a grin when he saw Dalla behind him, and went out. Vall saw his wife and the prisoner seated, and produced his cigarette case, handing it around.

"You're Zinganna; you're of the household of Councilman Salgath Trod, aren't you?" he asked.

"Housekeeper and hostess," the girl replied. "I am also his mistress."

Vall nodded, smiling. "Which confirms my long-standing respect for Councilman Salgath's exquisite taste."

"Why, thank you," she said. "But I doubt if I was brought here to receive compliments. Or was I?"

"No, I'm afraid not. Have you heard the newscasts of the past few hours concerning Councilman Salgath?"

She straightened in her seat, looking at him seriously.

"No. I and Nindrandigro and Calilla spent the evening on ServSec One-Six-Five. Councilman Salgath told me that he had some business and wanted them out of the apartment, and wanted me to keep an eye on them. We didn't hear any news at all." She hesitated. "Has anything . . . serious . . . happened?"

Vall studied her for a moment, then glanced at Dalla. There existed between himself and his wife a sort of vague, semitelepathic, rapport; they had never been able to transmit definite and exact thoughts, but they could clearly prehend one another's feelings and emotions. He was conscious, now, of Dalla's sympathy for the Proletarian girl.

"Zinganna, I'm going to tell you something that is being kept from the public," he said. "By doing so, I will make it necessary for us to detain you, at least for a few days. I hope you will forgive me, but I think you would forgive me less if I didn't tell you."

"Something's happened to him," she said, her eyes widening and her body tensing.

"Yes, Zinganna. At about 2010, this evening," he said, "Councilman Salgath was murdered."

"Oh!" She leaned back in the chair, closing her eyes. "He's dead?" Then, again, statement instead of question: "He's dead!"

For a long moment, she lay back in the chair, as though trying to reorient her mind to the fact of Salgath Trod's death, while Vall and Dalla sat watching her. Then she stirred, opened her eyes, looked at the cigarette in her fingers as though she had never seen it before, and leaned forward to stuff it into an ash receiver.

"Who did it?" she asked, the Stone Age savage who had been her ancestor not ten generations ago peeping out of her eyes.

"The men who actually used the needlers are dead," Vall told her. "I killed a couple of them myself. We still have to find the men who planned it. I'd hoped you'd want to help us do that, Zinganna."

He side-glanced to Dalla again; she nodded. The relationship between Zinganna and Salgath Trod hadn't been purely business with her; there had been some real affection. He told her what had happened, and when he reached the point at which Salgath Trod had called Tortha Karf to confess complicity in the slave trade, her lips tightened and she nodded.

"I was afraid it was something like that," she said. "For the last few days, well, ever since the news about the slave trade got out, he's been worried about something. I've always thought somebody had some kind of a hold over him. Different times in the past, he's done things so far against his own political best interests that I've had to believe he was being forced into them. Well, this time they tried to force him too far. What then?"

Vall continued the story. "So we're keeping this hushed up, for a while. The way we're letting it out, Salgath Trod is still alive, on Police Terminal, talking under narco-hypnosis."

She smiled savagely. "And they'll get frightened, and frightened men do foolish things," she finished. She hadn't been a politician's mistress for nothing. "What can I do to help?"

"Tell us everything you can," he said. "Maybe we can be able to take such actions as we would have taken if Salgath Trod had lived to talk to us."

"Yes, of course." She got another cigarette from the case Vall had laid on the table. "I think, though, that you'd better give me a narco-hypnosis. You want to be able to depend on what I'm going to tell you, and I want to be able to remember things exactly."

Vall nodded approvingly and turned to Dalla.

"Can you handle this, yourself?" he asked. "There's an audio-visual recorder on now; here's everything you need." He opened the drawers in the table to show her the narco-hypnotic equipment. "And the phone has a whisper mouthpiece; you can call out without worrying about your message getting into Zinganna's subconscious. Well, I'll see you when you're through; you bring Zinganna to Police Terminal; I'll probably be there."

He went out, closing the door behind him, and went down the hall, meeting the officer who had taken charge of the butler and housemaid.

"We're having trouble with them, sir," he said. "Hostile. Yelling about their rights, and demanding to see a representative of Proletarian Protective League."

Vall mentioned the Proletarian Protective League with unflattering vulgarity.

"If they don't coöperate, drag them out and inject them and question them anyhow," he said.

The detective-lieutenant looked worried. "We've been taking a pretty high hand with them as it is," he protested. "It's safer to kill a Citizen than bloody a Prole's nose; they have all sorts of laws to protect them."

"There are all sorts of laws to protect the Paratime Secret," Vall replied. "And I think there are one or two laws against murdering members of the Executive Council. In case P.P.L. makes any trouble, they aren't here; they have faithfully joined their beloved master in his refuge on PolTerm. But one or both of them work for the Organization."

"You're sure of that?"

"The Organization is too thorough not to have had a spy in Salgath's household. It wasn't Zinganna, because she's volunteered to talk to us under narco-hyp. So who does that leave?"

"Well, that's different; that makes them suspects." The lieutenant seemed relieved. "We'll pump that pair out right away."

When he got back to Tortha Karf's office, the Chief was awake, and doodling on his notepad with his multicolor pen. Vall looked at the pad and winced; the Chief was doodling bugs again — red ants with black legs, and blue-and-green beetles. Then he saw that the psychist, Nentrov Dard, was drinking straight 150-proof palm-rum.

"Well, tell me the worst," he said.

"Our boy's memory-obliterated," Nentrov Dard said, draining his glass and filling it again. "And he's plastered with pseudo-memories a foot thick. It'll be five or six ten-days before we can get all that stuff peeled off and get him unblocked. I put him to sleep and had him transposed to Police Terminal. I'm going there, myself, tomorrow morning, after I've had some sleep, and get to work on him. If you're hoping to get anything useful out of him in time to head off this Council crisis that's building up, just forget it."

"And that leaves us right back with our old friends, the Wizard Traders," Tortha Karf added. "And if they've decided to suspend activities on the Kholghoor Sector, too —" He began drawing a big blue and black spider in the middle of the pad.

Nentrov Dard crushed out his cigar, drank his rum, and got to his feet.

"Well, good night, Chief; Vall. If you decide to wake me up before 1000, send somebody you want to get rid of in a hurry." He walked around the deck and out the side door.

"I hope they don't," Vall said to Tortha Karf. "Really, though, I doubt if they do. This is their chance to pick up a lot of slaves cheaply; the Croutha are too busy to bother haggling. I'm going through to PolTerm, now; when Dalla and Zinganna get through, tell them to join me there."

On Police Terminal, he found Kostran Galth, the agent who had been selected to impersonate Salgath Trod. After calling Zulthran Torv, the mathematician in charge of the Computer Office and giving him the Esaron time-line designations and Nentrov Dard's ideas about them, he spent about an hour briefing Kostran Galth on the role he was to play. Finally, he undressed and went to bed on a couch in the rest room behind the office.

It was noon when he woke. After showering, shaving and dressing hastily, he went out to the desk for breakfast, which arrived while he was putting a call through to Ranthar Jard, at Nharkan Equivalent.

"Your idea paid off, Chief's Assistant," the Kholghoor SecReg Subchief told him. "The slaves gave us a lot of physical description data on the estate, and told us about new fields that had been cleared, and a dam this Lord Ghromdour was building to flood some new rice-paddies. We located a belt of about five parayears where these improvements had been made: we started boom-eranging the whole belt, time line by time line. So far, we have ten or fifteen pictures of the main square at Sohram showing Croutha with firearms, and pictures of Wizard Trader camps and conveyer heads on the same time lines. Here, let me show you; this is from an airboat over the forest outside the equivalent of Sohram."

There was no jungle visible when the view changed; nothing but clusters of steel towers and platforms and buildings that marked conveyer heads, and a large rectangle of red-and-white antigrav-buoys moored to warn air traffic out of the area being boomeranged. The pickup seemed to be pointed downward from the bow of an airboat circling at about ten thousand feet.

"Balls ready to go," a voice called, and then repeated a string of time-line designations. "Estimated return, 1820, give or take four minutes."

"Varth," Ranthar Jard said, evidently out of the boat's radio. "Your telecast is being beamed on Dhergabar Equivalent; Chief's

Assistant Verkan is watching. When do you estimate your next return?"

"Any moment, now, sir; we're holding this drop till they re-materialize."

Vall watched unblinkingly, his fork poised halfway to his mouth. Suddenly, about a thousand feet below the eye of the pickup, there was a series of blue flashes, and, an instant later, a blossoming of red-and-white parachutes, ejected from the photo-reconnaissance balls that had returned from the Kholghoor Sector.

"All right; drop away," the boat captain called. There was a gush, from underneath, of eight-inch spheres, their conductor-mesh twinkling golden-bright in the sunlight. They dropped in a tight cluster for a thousand or so feet and then flashed and vanished. From the ground, six or eight aircars rose to meet the descending parachutes and catch them.

The screen went cubist for a moment, and then Ranthar Jard's swarthy, wide-jawed face looked out of it again. He took his pipe from his mouth.

"We'll probably get a positive out of the batch you just saw coming in," he said. "We get one out of about every two drops."

"Message a list of the time-line designations you've gotten so far to Zulthran Torv, at Computer Office here," Vall said. "He's working on the Esaron Sector dope; we think a pattern can be established. I'll be seeing you in about five hours; I'm rocketing out of here as soon as I get a few more things cleared up here."

Zulthran Torv, normally cautious to the degree of pessimism, was jubilant when Vall called him.

"We have something, Vall," he said. "It is, roughly, what Dr. Nentrov suggested — each of the intervals between the designations is a very minute but very exact fraction of the difference between lesser designation and the base-line designation."

"You have the base-line designation?" Vall demanded.

"Oh, yes. That's what I was telling you. We worked that out from the designations you gave me." He recited it. "All the designations you gave me are —"

Vall wasn't listening to him. He frowned in puzzlement.

"That's not a Fifth Level designation," he said. "That's First Level!"

"That's correct. First Level Abzar Sector."

"Now why in blazes didn't anybody think of that before?" he

marveled, and as he did, he knew the answer. Nobody ever thought of the Abzar sector.

Twelve millennia ago, the world of the First Level had been exhausted; having used up the resources of their home planet, Mars, a hundred thousand years before, the descendants of the population that had migrated across space had repeated on the third planet the devastation of the fourth. The ancestors of Verkan Vall's people had discovered the principle of paratime transposition and had begun to exploit an infinity of worlds on other lines of probability. The people of the First Level Dwarma Sector, reduced by sheer starvation to a tiny handful, had abandoned their cities and renounced their technologies and created for themselves a farm-and-village culture without progress or change or curiosity or struggle or ambition, and a way of life in which every day was like every other day that had been or that would come.

The Abzar people had done neither. They had wasted their resources to the last, fighting bitterly over the ultimate crumbs, with fission bombs, and with muskets, and with swords, and with spears and clubs, and finally they had died out, leaving a planet of almost uniform desert dotted with vast empty cities which even twelve thousand years had hardly begun to obliterate.

So nobody on the Paratime Sector went to the Abzar Sector. There was nothing there — except a hiding-place.

"Well, message that to Subchief Ranthar Jard, Kholghoor Sector at Nharkan Equivalent, and to Subchief Vulthor, Esaron Sector, Novilan Equivalent," Vall said. "And be sure to mark what you send Vulthor, 'Immediate attention Deputy Subchief Skordran.'"

That reminded him of something; as soon as he was through with Zulthran, he got out an order in the name of Tortha Karf authorizing Skordran Kirv's promotion on a permanent basis and messaged it out. Something was going to have to be done with Vulthor Tharn, too. A promotion of course — say Deputy Bureau Chief. Hypno-Mech Tape Library at Dhergabar Home Time Line; there Vulthor's passion for procedure and his caution would be assets instead of liabilities. He called Vlasthor Arph, the Chief's Deputy assigned to him as adjutant.

"I want more troops from ServSec and IndSec," he said. "Go over the TO's and see what can be spared from where; don't strip any time line, but get a force of the order of about three divisions.

And locate all the big antigrav-equipped ship transposition docks on Commercial and Passenger Sectors, and a list of freighters and passenger ships that can be commandeered in a hurry. We think we've spotted the time line the Organization's using as a base. As soon as we raid a couple of places near Nharkan and Novilan Equivalents, we're going to move in for a planet-wide cleanup."

"I get it, Chief's Assistant. I do everything I can to get ready for a big move, without letting anything leak out. After you strike the first blow, there won't be any security problem, and the lid will be off. In the meantime, I make up a general plan, and alert all our own people. Right?"

"Right. And for your information, the base isn't Fifth Level; it's First Level Abzar." He gave the designation.

Vlasthor Arph chuckled. "Well, think of that! I'd even forgotten there was an Abzar Sector. Shall I tell the reporters that?"

"Fangs of Fasif, no!" Vall fairly howled. Then, curiously: "What reporters? How'd they get onto PolTerm?"

"About fifty or sixty news-service people Chief Tortha sent down here, this morning, with orders to prevent them from filing any stories from here but to let them cover the raids, when they come off. We were instructed to furnish them weapons and audio-visual equipment and vocowriters and anything else they needed, and —"

Vall grinned. "That was one I'd never thought of," he admitted. "The old fox is still the old fox. No, tell them nothing; we'll just take them along and show them. Oh, and where are Dr. Hadron Dalla and that girl of Salgath Trod's?"

"They're sleeping, now. Rest Room Eighteen."

Dalla and Zinganna were asleep on a big mound of silk cushions in one corner, their glossy black heads close together and Zinganna's brown arm around Dalla's white shoulder. Their faces were calmly beautiful in repose, and they smiled slightly, as though they were wandering through a happy dream. For a little while, Vall stood looking at them, then he began whistling softly. On the third or fourth bar, Dalla woke and sat up, waking Zinganna, and blinked at him perplexedly.

"What time is it?" she asked.

"About 1245," he told her.

"Ohhh! We just got to sleep," she said. "We're both bushed!"

"You had a hard time. Feel all right after your narco-hyp, Zinganna?"

"It wasn't so bad, and I had a nice sleep. And Dalla . . . Dr. Hadron, I mean —"

"Dalla," Vall's wife corrected. "Remember what I told you?"

"Dalla, then," Zinganna smiled. "Dalla gave me some hypno-treatment, too. I don't feel so badly about Trod, any more."

"Well, look, Zinganna. We're going to have a man impersonate Councilman Salgath on a telecast. The cosmeticians are making him over now. Would you find it too painful to meet him, and talk to him?"

"No, I wouldn't mind. I can criticize the impersonation; re-member, I knew Trod very well. You know, I was his hostess, too. I met many of the people with whom he was associated, and they know me. Would things look more convincing if I appeared on the telecast with your man?"

"It certainly would; it would be a great help!" he told her enthu-siastically. "Maybe you girls ought to get up, now. The telecast isn't till 1930, but there's a lot to be done getting ready."

Dalla yawned. "What I get, trying to be a cop," she said, then caught the other girl's hands and rose, pulling her up. "Come on, Zinna; we have to get to work!"

Vall rose from behind the reading-screen in Ranthar Jard's office, stretching his arms over his head. For almost an hour, he had sat there pushing buttons and twiddling selector and magnification-adjustment knobs, looking at the pictures the Kholghoor-Nharkan cops had taken with auto-return balls dropped over the spatial equivalent of Sohram. One set of pictures, taken at two thousand feet, showed the central square of the city. The effects of the Croutha sack were plainly visible; so were the captives herded together under guard like cattle. By increasing magnification, he looked at groups of the barbarian conquerors, big men with blond or reddish-brown hair, in loose shirts and baggy trousers and rough cowhide buskins. Many of them wore bowl-shaped helmets, some had shirts of ring-mail, all of them carried long straight swords with cross-hilts, and about half of them had pistols thrust through their belts or muskets slung from their shoulders.

The other set of pictures showed the Wizard Trader camps and conveyer heads. In each case, a wide oval had been burned out in the jungle, probably with heavy-duty heat guns. The camps were surrounded with stout wire-mesh fence: in each there were a number of metal prefab-huts, and an inner fenced slave-pen. A trail had been cut from each to a similarly cleared circle farther back in the forest, and in the centers of one or two of these circles he saw the actual conveyer domes. There was a great deal of activity in all of them, and he screwed the magnification-adjustment to the limit to scrutinize each human figure in turn. A few of the men, he was sure, were First Level Citizens; more were either Proles or out-timers. Quite a few of them were of a dark, heavy-featured, black-bearded type.

"Some of these fellows look like Second Level Khiftans," he said. "Rush an individual picture of each one, maximum magnification consistent with clarity, to Dhergabar Equivalent to be transposed to Home Time Line. You get all the dope from Zulthran Torv?"

"Yes; Abzar Sector," Ranthar Jard said. "I'd never have thought of that. Wonder why they used that series system, though. I'd have tried to spot my operations as completely at random as possible."

"Only thing they could have done," Vall said. "When we get hold of one of their conveyers, we're going to find the control panel's just a mess of arbitrary symbols, and there'll be something like a computer-machine built into the control cabinet, to select the right time line whenever a dial's set or a button pushed, and the only way that could be done would be by establishing some kind of a numerical series. And we were trustingly expecting to locate their base from one of their conveyers! Why, if we give all those people in the pictures narco-hyps, we won't learn the base-line designation; none of them will know it. They just go where the conveyers take them."

"Well, we're all set now," Ranthar Jard said. "I have a plan of attack worked out; subject to your approval, I'm ready to start implementing it now." He glanced at his watch. "The Salgath telecast is over, on Home Time Line, and in a little while, a transcript will be on this time line. Want to watch it here, sir?"

The telecast screen in the living room of Tortha Karf's town apartment was still on; in it, a girl with bright red hair danced slowly to soft music against a background of shifting color. The four men who sat in a semicircle facing it sipped their drinks and watched idly.

"Ought to be getting some sort of public reaction soon," Tortha Karf said, glancing at his watch.

"Well, I'll have to admit, it was done convincingly," Zostha Olv, the Chief Interoffice Coördinator, admitted grudgingly. "I'd have believed it, if I hadn't known the real facts."

"Shooting it against the background of those wide windows was smart," Lovranth Rolk said. "Every schoolchild would recognize that view of the rocketport as being on Police Terminal. And including that girl Zinganna; that was a real masterpiece!"

"I've met her, a few times," Elbraz Vark, the Political Liaison Assistant, said. "Isn't she lovely!"

"Good actress, too," Tortha Karf said. "It's not easy to impersonate yourself."

"Well, Kostran Galth did a fine job of acting, too," Lovranth Rolk said. "That was done to perfection — the distinguished politician, supported by his loyal mistress, bravely facing the disgraceful end of his public career."

"You know, I believe I could get that girl a booking with one of the big theatrical companies. Now that Salgath's dead, she'll need somebody to look after her."

"What sharp, furry ears you have, Mr. Elbraz!" Zostha Olv grunted.

The music stopped as though cut off with a knife, and the slim girl with the red hair vanished in a shatter of many colors. When the screen cleared, one of the announcers was looking out of it.

"We interrupt the program for an important newscast of a sensational development in the Salgath affair," he said. "Your next speaker will be Yandar Yadd —"

"I thought you'd managed to get that blabbermouth transposed to PolTerm," Zostha said.

"He wouldn't go." Tortha Karf replied. "Said it was just a trick to get him off Home Time Line during the Council crisis."

Yandar Yadd had appeared on the screen as the pickup swung about.

". . . Recording ostensibly made by Councilman Salgath on Police Terminal Time Line, and telecast on Home Time Line an hour ago. Well, I don't know who he was, but I now have positive proof that he definitely was not Salgath Trod!"

"We're sunk!" Zostha Olv grunted. "He'd never make a statement like that unless he could prove it."

". . . Something suspicious about the whole thing, from the beginning," the newsman was saying. "So I checked. If you recall, the actor impersonating Salgath gestured rather freely with his hands, in imitation of a well-known mannerism of the real Salgath Trod; at one point, the ball of his right thumb was presented directly to the pickup. Here's a still of that scene."

He stepped aside, revealing a viewscreen behind him; when he pressed a button, the screen lighted; on it was a stationary picture of Kostran Galth as Salgath Trod, his right hand raised in front of him.

"Now watch this. I'm going to step up the magnification, slowly, so that you can be sure there's no substitution. Camera a little closer, Trath!"

The screen in the background seemed to advance, until it filled the entire screen. Yandar Yadd was still talking, out of the picture; a metal-tipped pointer came into the picture, touching the right thumb, which grew larger and larger until it was the only thing visible.

"Now here," Yandar Yadd's voice continued. "Any of you who are familiar with the ancient science of dactyloscopy will recognize this thumb as having the ridge-pattern known as a 'twin loop.' Even with the high degree of magnification possible with the microgrid screen, we can't bring out the individual ridges, but the pattern is unmistakable. I ask you to memorize that image, while I show you another right thumb print, this time a certified photo-copy of the thumb print of the real Salgath Trod." The magnification was reduced a little, a card was moved into the picture, and it was stepped up again. "See, this thumb print is of the type known as a 'tented arch.' Observe the difference."

"That does it!" Zostha Olv cried. "Karf, for the first and last time, let me remind you that I opposed this lunacy from the beginning. Now, what are we going to do next?"

"I suggest that we get to Headquarters as soon as we can," Tortha Karf said. "If we wait too long, we may not be able to get in."

Yandar Yadd was back on the screen, denouncing Tortha Karf passionately. Tortha went over and snapped it off.

"I suggest we transpose to PolTerm," Lovranth Rolk said. "It won't be so easy for them to serve a summons on us there."

"You can go to PolTerm if you want to," Tortha Karf retorted. "I'm going to stay here and fight back, and if they try to serve me with a summons, they'd better send a robot for a process server."

"Fight back!" Zostha Olv echoed. "You can't fight the Council and the whole Management! They'll tear you into inch bits!"

"I can hold them off till Vall's able to raid those Abzar Sector bases," Tortha Karf said. He thought for a moment. "Maybe this is all for the best, after all. If it distracts the Organization's attention —"

"I wish we could have made a boomerang-ball reconnaissance," Ranthar Jard was saying, watching one of the viewscreens, in which a film, taken from an airboat transposed to an adjoining Abzar sector time line, was being shown. The boat had circled over the Ganges, a mere trickle between wide, deeply cut banks, and was crossing a gullied plain, sparsely grown with thornbush. "The base ought to be about there, but we have no idea what sort of changes this gang has made."

"Well, we couldn't: we didn't dare take the chance of it being spotted. This has to be a complete surprise. It'll be about like the other place, the one the slaves described. There won't be any permanent buildings. This operation only started a few months ago, with the Croutha invasion; it may go on for four or five months, till the Croutha have all their surplus captives sold off. That country," he added, gesturing at the screen, "will be flooded out when the rains come. See how it's suffered from flood-erosion. There won't be a thing there that can't be knocked down and transposed out in a day or so."

"I wish you'd let me go along," Ranthar Jard worried.

"We can't do that, either," Vall said. "Somebody's got to be in charge here, and you know your own people better than I do. Beside, this won't be the last operation like this. Next time, I'll have to stay on Police Terminal and command from a desk; I want first-hand experience with the outtime end of the job, and this is the only way I can get it."

He watched the four police-girls who were working at the big terrain board showing the area of the Police Terminal time line around them. They had covered the miniature buildings and platforms and towers with a fine mesh, at a scale-equivalent of fifty feet; each intersection marked the location of a three-foot conveyer ball, loaded with a sleep-gas bomb and rigged with an automatic detonator which would explode it and release the gas as soon as it rematerialized on the Abzar Sector. Higher, on stiff wires that raised them to what represented three thousand feet, were the disks that stood for ten hundred-foot conveyers; they would carry squads of Paratime Police in aircars and thirty-foot air boats. There was a ring of big two-hundred-foot conveyers a mile out; they would carry the armor and the airborne infantry and the little two-man scooters of the air-cavalry, from the Service and Industrial Sectors. Directly over the spatial equivalent of the Kholghoor Sector Wizard Traders' conveyers was the single disk of Verkan Vall's command conveyer, at a represented five thousand feet, and in a half-mile circle around it were the five news service conveyers.

"Where's the ship-conveyer?" he asked.

"Actually it's on antigrav about five miles north of here," one of the girls said. "Representationally, about where Subchief Ranthar's standing."

Another girl added a few more bits to the network that represented the sleep-gas bombs and stepped back, taking off her earphones.

"Everything's in place, now, Assistant Verkan," she told him.

"Good. I'm going aboard, now," he said. "You can have it, Jard."

He shook hands with Ranthar Jard, who moved to the switch which would activate all the conveyers simultaneously, and accepted the good wishes of the girls at the terrain board. Then he walked to the mesh-covered dome of the hundred-foot conveyer, with the five news service conveyers surrounding it in as regular a circle as the buildings and towers of the regular conveyer heads would permit. The members of his own detail, smoking and chatting outside, saw him and started moving inside; so did the news people. A public-address speaker began yelping, in a hundred voices all over the area, warning those who were going with the conveyers to get aboard. He went in through a door, between two aircars, and on to the central control-desks, going up to a visiscreen over which somebody had crayoned "Novilan EQ." It gave him a view, over the shoulder of a man in the uniform of a field agent third class, of the interior of a conveyer like his own.

"Hello, Assistant Verkan," a voice came out of the speaker under the screen, as the man moved his lips. "Deputy Skordran! Here's Chief's Assistant Verkan, now!"

Skordran Kirv moved in front of the screen as the operator got up from his stool.

"Hello, Vall; we're all set to move out as soon as you give the word," he said. "We're all in position on antigrav."

"That's smart work. We've just finished our gas-bomb net," Vall said. "Going on antigrav now," he added, as he felt the dome lift. "I hope you won't be too disappointed if you draw a blank on your end."

"We realize that they've closed out the whole Esaron Sector," Skordran Kirv, eight thousand odd miles away, replied. "We're taking in a couple of ships; we're going to make a survey all up the coast. There are a lot of other sectors where slaves can be sold in this area."

In the outside viewscreen, tuned to a slowly rotating pickup on the top of a tower spatially equivalent with a room in a tall building on Second Level Triplanetary Empire Sector, he could see his own conveyer rising vertically, with the news conveyers following, and the troop conveyers, several miles away, coming into position. Finally, they were all placed; he reported the fact to Skordran Kirv and then picked up a hand-phone.

"Everybody ready for transposition?" he called. "On my count. Thirty seconds . . . Twenty seconds . . . Fifteen seconds . . . Five seconds . . . Four seconds . . . Three seconds . . . Two seconds . . . One second, *out!*"

All the screens went gray. The inside of the dome passed into another space-time continuum, even into another kind of space-time. The transposition would take half an hour; that seemed to be the time needed to build up and collapse the transposition field, regardless of the paratemporal distance covered. The dome above and around them vanished; the bare, tower-forested, building-dotted world of Police Terminal vanished, too, into the uniform green of the uninhabited Fifth Level. A planet could take pretty good care of itself, he thought, if people would only leave it alone. Then he began to see the fields and villages of Fourth Level. Cities appeared and vanished, growing higher and vaster as they went across the more civilized Third Level. One was under air attack — there was almost never a paratemporal transposition which did not run through some scene of battle.

He unbuckled his belt and took off his boots and tunic; all around him, the others were doing the same. Sleep-gas didn't have to be breathed; it could enter the nervous system by any orifice or lesion, even a pore or a scratch. A spacesuit was the only protection. One of the detectives helped him on with his metal and plastic armor; before sealing his gauntlets, he reciprocated the assistance, then checked the needler and blaster and the long batonlike ultrasonic paralyzer on his belt and made sure that the radio and soundphones in his helmet were working. He hoped that the frantic efforts to gather several thousand spacesuits onto Police Terminal from the Industrial and Commercial and Interplanetary Sectors hadn't started rumors which had gotten to the ears of some of the Organization's ubiquitous agents.

The country below was already turning to the parched browns and yellows of the Abzar Sector. There was not another of the conveyers in sight, but electronic and mechanical lag in the individual controls and even the distance-difference between them and the central radio control would have prevented them from going into transposition at the same fractional microsecond. The recon-details began piling into their cars. Then the red light overhead winked to green, and the dome flickered and solidified into cold, inert metal. The screens lighted up again, and Vall could see Skordran Kirv, across Asia and the Pacific, getting into his helmet. A dot of light in the center of the underview screen widened as the mesh under the conveyer irised open around the pickup.

Below, the Organization base — big rectangles of fenced slave pens, with metal barracks inside; the huge circle of the Kholghoor Sector conveyer-head building, and a smaller structure that must house conveyers to other Abzar Sector time lines; the work-shops and living quarters and hangars and warehouses and docks — was wreathed in white-green mist. The ring of conveyers at three thousand feet were opening and spewing out aircars and airboats, farther away, the greater ring of heavy conveyers were unloading armored and shielded combat-craft. An aircar which must have been above the reach of the gas was streaking away toward the west, with three police cars after it. As he watched, the air around it fairly sizzled blue with the rays of neutron disruption blasters, and then it blew apart. The three police cars turned and came back more slowly. The three-thousand-ton passenger ship which had been hastily fitted with armament was circling about; the great dock conveyer which had brought it was gone, transposed back to Police Terminal to pick up another ship.

He recorded a message announcing the arrival of the task-force, pulled out the tape and sealed it in a capsule, and put the capsule in a mesh message ball, attaching it to a couple of wires and flipping a switch. The ball flashed and vanished, leaving the wires cleanly sheared off. When it got back to Police Terminal, half an hour later, it would rematerialize, eject a parachute, and turn on a whistle to call attention to itself. Then he sealed on his helmet, climbed into an aircar, and turned on his helmet-radio to speak to the driver. The car lifted a few inches, floated out an open port, and dived downward.

He landed at the big conveyer-head building. There were spaces for fifty conveyers around it, and all but eight of them were in place. One must have arrived since the gas bombs burst; it was crammed with senseless Kharanda slaves. A couple of Paratime Police officers were towing a tank of sleep-gas around on an antigrav-lifter, maintaining the proper concentration in case any more came in. At the smaller conveyer building, there were no conveyers, only a number of red-lined fifty-foot circles around a central two-hundred-foot circle. The Organization personnel there had been dragged outside, and a group of paracops were sealing it up, installing robot watchmen, and preparing to flood it with gas. At the slave pens, a string of two-hundred-foot conveyers, having unloaded soldiers and fighting-gear, were coming in to take on unconscious slaves for transposition to Police Terminal. Aircars and airboats were bringing in gassed slavers; they were being shackled and dumped into the slave barracks; as soon as the gas cleared and they could be brought back to consciousness, they would be narco-hypnotized and questioned.

He had finished a tour of the warehouses, looking at the kegs of gunpowder and the casks of brandy, the piles of pig lead, the stacks of cases containing muskets. These must have all come from some low-order handcraft time line. Then there were swords and hatchets and knives that had been made on Industrial Sector — the

Organization must be getting them through some legitimate trading company — and mirrors and perfumes and synthetic fiber textiles and cheap jewelry, of similar provenance. It looked as though this stuff had been brought in by ship from somewhere else on this time line; the warehouses were too far from the conveyers and right beside the ship dock —

There was a tremendous explosion somewhere. Vall and the men with him ran outside, looking about, the sound-phones of their helmets giving them no idea of the source of the sound. One of the policemen pointed, and Vall's eyes followed his arm. The ship that had been transposed in in the big conveyer was falling, blown in half; as he looked, both sections hit the ground several miles away. A strange ship, a freighter, was coming in fast, and as he watched, a blue spark winked from her bow as a heavy-duty blaster was activated. There was another explosion, overhead; they all ran for shelter as Vall's command-conveyer disintegrated into falling scrap-metal. At once, all the other conveyers which were on antigrav began flashing and vanishing. That was the right, the only, thing to do, he knew. But it was leaving him and his men isolated and under attack.

"So that was it," Dalgroth Sorn, the Paratime Commissioner for Security said, relieved when Tortha Karf had finished.

"Yes, and I'll repeat it under narco-hyp, too," Tortha Karf added.

"Oh, don't talk that way, Karf," Dalgroth Sorn scolded. He was at least a century Tortha Karf's senior; he had the face of an elderly and sore-toothed lion. "You wanted to keep this prisoner under wraps till you could mind-pump him, and you wanted the Organization to think Salgath was alive and talking. I approve both. But —"

He gestured to the viewscreen across the room, tuned to a pickup back of the Speaker's chair in the Council Chamber. Tortha Karf turned a knob to bring the sound volume up.

"Well. I'm raising this point," a member from the Management seats in the center was saying, "because these earlier charges of illegal arrest and illegal detention are part and parcel with the charges growing out of the telecast last evening."

"Well, that telecast was a fake; that's been established," somebody on the left heckled.

"Councilman Salgath's confession on the evening of One-Six-

Two Day wasn't a fake, the Management supporter, Nanthav Skov, retorted.

"Well, then why was it necessary to fake the second one?"

A light began winking on the big panel in front of the Speaker, Asthar Varn.

"I recognize Councilman Hasthor Flan," Asthar said.

"I believe I can construct a theory that will explain that," Hasthor Flan said. "I suggest that when the Paratime Police were questioning Councilman Salgath under narco-hypnosis, he made statements incriminating either the Paratime Police as a whole or some member of the Paratime Police whom Tortha Karf had to protect — say somebody like Assistant Verkan. So they just killed him, and made up this impostor —"

Tortha Karf began, alphabetically, to blaspheme every god he had ever heard of. He had only gotten as far as a Fourth Level deity named Allah when a red light began flashing in front of Asthar Varn, and the voice of a page-robot, amplified, roared:

"Point of special urgency! Point of special urgency! It has been requested that the news telecast screen be activated at once, with playback to 1107. An important bulletin has just come in from Nagorabar, Home Time Line, on the Indian subcontinent —"

"You can stop swearing, now, Karf," Dalgroth Sorn grinned. "I think this is it."

Kostran Galth sat on the edge of the couch, with one arm around Zinganna's waist; on the other side of him, Hadron Dalla lay at full length, her elbows propped and her chin in her hands. The screen in front of them showed a fading sunset, although it was only a little past noon at Dhergabar Equivalent. A dark ship was coming slowly in against the red sky; in the center of a wire-fenced compound a hundred-foot conveyer hung on antigrav twenty feet from the ground, and beyond, a long metal prefab-shed was spilling light from open doors and windows.

"That crowd that was just taken in won't be finished for a couple of hours," a voice was saying. "I don't know how much they'll be able to tell; the psychists say they're all telling about the same stories. What those stories are, of course, I'm not able to repeat. After the trouble caused by a certain news commentator who shall be nameless — he's not connected with this news service,

I'm happy to say — we're all leaning over backward to keep from breaking Paratime Police security.

"One thing; shortly after the arrival of the second ship from Police Terminal — and believe me, that ship came in just in the nick of time! — the dead Abzar city which the criminals were using as their main base for this time line, and from which they launched the air attack against us, was located, and now word has come in that it is entirely in the hands of the Paratime Police. Personally, I doubt if a great deal of information has been gotten from any prisoners taken there. The lengths to which this Organization went to keep their own people in ignorance is simply unbelievable."

A man appeared for a moment in the lighted doorway of the shed, then stepped outside.

"Look!" Dalla cried. "There's Vall!"

"There's Assistant Verkan, now," the commentator agreed. "Chief's Assistant, would you mind saying a few words, here? I know you're a busy man, sir, but you are also the public hero of Home Time Line, and everybody will be glad if you say something to them —"

Tortha Karf sealed the door of the apartment behind them, then activated one of the robot servants and sent it gliding out of the room for drinks. Verkan Vall took off his belt and holster and laid them aside, then dropped into a deep chair with a sigh of relief. Dalla advanced to the middle of the room and stood looking about in surprised delight.

"Didn't expect this, from the mess outside?" Vall asked. "You know, you really are on the paracops, now. Nobody off the Force knows about this hideout of the Chief's."

"You'd better find a place like this, too," Tortha Karf advised. "From now on, you'll have about as much privacy at that apartment in Turquoise Towers as you'd enjoy on the stage of Dhergabar Opera House."

"Just what is my new position?" Vall asked, hunting his cigarette case out of his tunic. "Duplicate Chief of Paratime Police?"

*   *   *

The robot came back with three tall glasses and a refrigerated decanter on its top. It stopped in front of Tortha Karf and slewed around on its treads; he filled a glass and sent it to the chair where

Dalla had seated herself; when she got a drink, she sent it to Vall. Vall sent if back to Tortha Karf, who turned it off.

"No; you have the modifier in the wrong place. You're Chief of Duplicate Paratime Police. You take the setup you have now, and expand it; continue the present lines of investigation, and be ready to exploit anything new that comes up. You won't bother with any of this routine flying-saucer-scare stuff; just handle the Organization business. That'll keep you busy for a long time, I'm afraid."

"I notice you slammed down on the first Council member who began shouting about how you'd wiped out the Great Paratemporal Crime-Ring," Vall said.

"Yes. It isn't wiped out, and it won't be wiped out for a long time. I shall be unspeakably delighted if, when I turn my job over to you, you have it wiped out. And even then, there'll be a loose end to pick up every now and then till you retire."

"We have Council and the Management with us, now," Vall said. "This was the first secret session of Executive Council in over two thousand years. And I thought I'd drop dead when they passed that motion to submit themselves to narco-hypnosis."

"A few Councilmen are going to drop dead before they can be narco-hypped," Dalla prophesied over the rim of her glass.

"A few have already. I have a list of about a dozen of them who have had fatal accidents or committed suicide, or just died or vanished since the news of your raid broke. Four of them I saw, in the screen, jump up and run out as soon as the news came in, on One-Six-Five Day. And a lot of other people; our friend Yandar Yadd's dropped out of sight, for one. You heard what we got out of those servants of Salgath Trod's?"

"I didn't," Dalla said. "What?"

"Both spies for the Organization. They reported to a woman named Farilla, who ran a fortune-telling parlor in the Prole district. Her occult powers didn't warn her before we sent a squad of plain-clothes men for her. That was an entirely illegal arrest, by the way, but it netted us a list of about three hundred prominent political, business and social persons whose servants have been reporting to her. She thought she was working for a telecast gossipist."

"That's why we have a new butler, darling," Vall interrupted. "Kandagro was reporting on us."

"Who did she pass the reports on to?" Dalla asked.

Tortha Karf beamed. "She thinks more like a cop every time I talk to her," he told Vall. "You better appoint her your Special Assistant. Why, about 1800 every day, some Prole would come in, give the recognition sign, and get the day's accumulation. We only got one of them, a fourteen-year-old girl. We're having some trouble getting her deconditioned to a point where she can be hypnotized into talking; by the time we do, they'll have everything closed out, I suppose. What's the latest from Abzar Sector? I missed the last report in the rush to get to this Council session."

"All stalled. We're still boomeranging the sector, but it's about five billion time-lines deep, and the pattern for the Kholghoor and Esaron Sectors doesn't seem to apply. I think they have a lot of these Abzar time lines close together, and they get from one to another via some terminal on Fifth Level."

Tortha Karf nodded. It was impossible to make a transposition of less than ten parayears — a hundred thousand time lines. It was impossible that the field could build and collapse that soon.

"We also think that this Abzar time line was only used for the Croutha-Wizard Trader operation. Nothing we found there was more than a couple of months old; nothing since the last rainy season in India, for instance. Everything was cleaned out on Skordran Kirv's end."

"Tell him to try the Mississippi, Missouri and Ohio Valleys," Tortha Karf said. "A lot of those slaves are sure to have been sold to Second Level Khiftan Sector."

"Well, it looks as though our vacation's out the window for a long time," Dalla said resignedly.

"Why don't you and Vall go to my farm, on Fifth Level Sicily," Tortha Karf suggested. "I own the whole island, on that time line, and you can always be reached in a hurry if anything comes up."

"We could have as much fun there as on the Dwarma Sector," Dalla said. "Chief, could we take a couple of friends along?"

"Well, who?"

"Zinganna and Kostran Galth," she replied. "They've gotten interested in one another; they're talking about a tentative marriage."

"It'll have to be mighty tentative," Vall said. "Kostran Galth can't marry a Prole."

"She won't be a Prole very long. I'm going to adopt her as my sister."

Tortha Karf looked at her sharply. "You sure you know what you're doing, Dalla?" he asked.

"Of course I'm sure. I know that girl better than she knows herself. I narco-hypped her, remember. Zinna's the kind of a sister I've always wished I'd had."

"Well, that's all right then. But about this marriage. She was in love with Salgath Trod," Tortha Karf said. "Now, she's identifying Agent Kostran with him —"

"She was in love with the kind of man Salgath could have been if he hadn't gotten into this Organization filth," Dalla replied. "Galth is that kind of a man. They'll get along all right."

"Well, she'll qualify on IQ and general psych rating for Citizenship. I'll say that. And she's the kind of girl I like to see my boys take up with. Like you, Dalla. Yes, of course; take them along with you. Sicily's big enough that two couples won't get in each others' way."

A phone-robot, its slender metal stem topped by a metal globe, slid into the room on its ball-rollers, moving falteringly, like a blind man. It could sense Tortha Karf's electro-encephalic wave-patterns, but it was having trouble locating the source. They all sat motionless, waiting; finally it came over to Tortha Karf's chair and stopped. He unhooked the phone and held a lengthy whispered conversation with somebody before replacing it.

"Now, there," he explained to Dalla. "That's a sample of why we have to set up this duplicate organization. Revolution just broke out at Ftanna, on Third Level Tsorshay Sector; a lot of our people, mostly tourists and students, are cut off from their conveyers by street fighting. Going to be a pretty bloody business getting them out." He finished his drink and got to his feet. "Sit still; I just have to make a few screen-calls. Send the robot for something to eat, Vall. I'll be right back."

THE END

www.ingramcontent.com/pod-product-compliance
Lightning Source LLC
Chambersburg PA
CBHW030537180626
46810CB00005B/1912